Fallen Honor

William Price Jr

Cover Design by ebooklaunch.com

ISBN: 979-8-9986147-2-9

Other Books by William Price Jr:

The Fallen Angel Series
Fallen Love
Fallen Justice
Fallen Honor

The Master of Fate Series
Into the Northlands
The Northern Keep
The Western Empire
The Eastern War

For Eric and David,
my brothers who betrayed me,
and who I struggle to forgive.

1

The closet was supposed to be a punishment. If he misbehaved, if he spoke out of turn, or did not answer correctly, they put him in the closet. If her dared to ask for more food, or was not appreciative enough for the scraps, they put him in the closet. If her asked to use the restroom, or if he soiled himself, they put him in the closet. If he did anything they did not like, or if he did nothing at all, they put him in the closet. The closet was supposed to be a punishment.

They did not know that he preferred the closet. The darkness was safe; he could not see the smoking, injecting, or fornicating in the closet. The narrow walls were comforting; they were the closest thing he knew to a loving embrace. The quiet was a relief; there were no shouts, no screams, no sobbing or begging in the closet. He was alone in the closet; there were no beatings, no cursing or blames. He only had a few stinking, rotting pillows, but this was more than he had outside the closet.

They called him boy. They knew the name he wanted to be called, but they only ever called him boy when they weren't cursing him. He was not a little boy, though. Little boys were not treated like they treated him. He looked like one, but only on the outside. Once, he had a shining light within him, but now there was only darkness, darkness and a secret. He was short as most little boys were, and his body was undeveloped. They sometimes called him a girl, and let him be used as one. His voice was light, when he used it, when he could still remember how to pray. His face was smooth and pale, when not covered in bruises. His frame was thin, though much of that was from a lack of food. On the surface, he seemed like any other child, barely approaching the difficult transition into adulthood. But that was only on the surface.

They looked at him and saw what they wanted to see, what they expected to see. They looked at him and saw a tiny version of themselves. Within him, they saw a shadow of innocence, something they had lost long ago. They heard a voice lacking experience, lacking the defeats and misery of a lifetime of sin, of a life within a fallen world. They looked at him, and they saw the prison in which they had condemned themselves. They hated what they saw in him, and punished it.

His life had not always been darkness and the closet. Once, he had been happy. He remembered having a family, siblings and friends who loved him and who he loved. They had a wonderful home, filled with music and joy. Once, he and his siblings had helped people, easing the suffering that came with life and living. He had enjoyed helping and being with his family.

But, one day, people had come for him. They had said a difficult thing had needed to be done. They had forced him into darkness, and placed within this soft body a terrible secret. They had locked him away from his family. They had taken from him music and laughter. They had passed him from one group to another, always greedy for his secret. Time had become strange to him; he did not recognize days or nights or months or years. Always there was only the safety of darkness, and the horrible pain of light.

He was stolen. The people who kept him, who passed him along to their friends, who forever kept him moving from one dark place to another, tried to keep him, but could not. Others wanted his secret. They took him away and hurt him. They demanded what he had, what he was. Others stole him away, also hungry for him and his secret. He became a thing, a trophy or a toy, stolen, recovered, lost, found, fought over, hated and desired. He was sold and ransomed. He was freed and imprisoned. He was a prize. The one thing he never was, never allowed to be, was a little boy.

And now, he was in the closet. He could not remember how long, this time, he had been in the closet. The ones who had him now were neglectful. They had business, and called him, "the package." They did not care if he ate. They did not care if he slept. They took him from one closet to the next. They beat him if he did not move fast enough, or if they thought he was resisting. Some dark part of his mind found this funny: as though he had any will left to resist.

He had tried to escape. Long ago, or perhaps only last night, they had fallen asleep, lost in drugs and flesh. Those who were supposed to be watching him forgot their duty. He had slipped away. He had seen a number, written on the side of a building. He had seen a phone, left unattended by its owner, even as he had been left unattended by his owners. He had used the phone to call the number. A girl had answered, and he had begged for help. She had promised to help, to find him. But then, they had found him again, and put him back into the closet.

A noise caught his attention. He moved to the door of his closet. This newest place once housed families, but that was long ago. The shelves were bare and rotting, just as the rest of this former home was. They had blindfolded him before bringing him here, and beat him for escaping, for costing them time and money and effort. Lack of sight meant little though, since the darkness was so comforting. His nose had detected the reek of mildew and unwashed bodies as they dragged him to this newest closet. His ears had detected the creak of dying wood and Humans lost to chemical despair. His nearly-numb flesh recoiled from hands that were purposeful and greedy, hateful and hopeless. This house had once been a place of love and comfort, but now it was a den of suffering, of soul-death and exploitation.

They had put him in this closet a while ago. His unwanted body was weakening, having not been fed in a very long while. His stomach ached, this throat burned, and he could barely keep his small eyes open. His captors seemed not to care, however.

Worse than the indifference, the darkness, and the painful reminders of how weak his prison of flesh was, were the sounds that reminded him of what he had once been. Gasped moans, not of pleasure, but of hunger and fear and despair, drifted in from under the door. Grunts accompanied the slap of flesh on flesh. He knew these sounds from his time before, when he and his family had helped people. He recognized what was supposed to be love, what was supposed to grant some tiny approximation of compassion. He was not a little boy, because he recognized and understood the sounds of exploitation, domination, and vile corruption. And this fornication was not the only evil that revealed itself during his newest imprisonment.

Chemical smells stung at his small nostrils. Desperate whispers, stumbling steps, and trembling begging all suggested the sale and consumption of narcotics. Again something meant to offer comfort and support had been perverted. One of the Chorus, he did not remember which, had taught the earliest generations of Humans how to ease their physical suffering with plants, to cure sickness and sooth pain. They had needed only a handful of years before that pharmica had been corrupted. Greater and greater evil was brewed by chemists; poison was crafted and labeled as bliss. He could not tell what form of toxins were being sold here; there were so many now, like all the sufferings Humans inflicted upon one another.

This was the worst of his imprisonment. Not only within this closet, but within this ridiculous adolescent body. He had spent countless centuries trying to bring comfort to those abused by what was supposed to be one of their few comforts in their short lives. This had been his purpose, the Word used to form him into existence: mercy. He had spent countless centuries witnessing the worst suffering these creatures caused one another, trying to bring whatever comfort he could, but knowing that only Death offered a true release.

The strange, new sound was growing. He leaned down, not needing to go far in his useless young form, pressing his small ear to the gap separating door from frame. He needed a moment before realizing that it was not a sound, but a feeling. The shred of connection to the aether they had left him, more punishment for its echo of familiarity, detected the approach of another. One like him, but different. Not another of the Fallen, but something close. Some years had passed since he had felt the sympathetic vibration within his unwanted soul, harmonizing with another lost, former Celestial. He had spent most of his time on Earth avoiding the other Fallen, for fear they would discover what he carried. Ironic, since it was a group of Humans who had learned of his burden and now did what he feared the Fallen would do: seek to extract it.

Voices approached from down a hall. Most were those of his captors: little more than grunts of attempted strength. They were criminals, he recognized. Predators seeking to extract as much profit and suffering from their neighbors as possible. They were like any other scavengers, barking, trying to intimidate, especially when confronted by a greater predator. There was another voice among the Humans. Soft, light, almost musical. The fragrance of flowers and peace briefly caressed his nose, trying to push away the unwashed stench of the rotting prison. A woman then. *No, her step is too light, a girl?*

"I'm sure we can make you a better offer," she was saying to the scavengers. "If it's only about money, we can offer more."

They had entered the room outside his closet. He leaned even lower, trying to hear, to sense, to understand what was happening. The other he had first sensed was nearby, but not with the small group that had entered. There was someone with them, though, some heavy echo near the girl.

"Plus," the girl-voice was continuing, "You don't have to worry about us stabbing you in the back. Unlike the *Drest-Vidar*, we deal fairly."

The *Drest-Vidar*, he nodded to himself. The flesh-peddlers who had first captured him. The inheritors of Solomon's misguided attempts to control Celestials. A cabal of spell-casters who had learned of what he carried. They had held him, tortured him, working their childish magics with no success.

"We don't deal with the *Drest-Vidar*," the voice of one of his new captors argued.

"Be hard to," a new voice replied. This one was deep and hard. It pushed through the air, shouldering aside any other sound. It felt like a storm just off the horizon, impatient to unleash itself upon the world.

"Yeah," the captor agreed. "We'd heard they'd all been arrested or killed. Was that you?"

"Do you care?" There was something familiar about that voice, something that called to him. It felt much like when Humans caught a scent that briefly brought their souls back to a grandmother's kitchen. Something in that voice called to him, to a time before his prison of a boy's flesh.

"Not really. I never like dealing with them anyway. They gave me the creeps."

"So," the girl's voice broke in. He could almost feel her agitation with the deeper voice, her insistence on asserting control over it. "Can we talk business?"

"Not with me," the captor's voice answered. "You've got to talk to the boss." Oddly, when the captor said the word boss, the tone shifted slightly, becoming impatient.

"And who's the boss?" the girl asked politely.

"That would be me, fuckers." He recognized this voice. It came infrequently, but was noticeable. It carried the accent of further south, but little evidence of education or refinement. That voice came with a very light step, so much so that he had thought it belonged to a child. The tiny voice, though, spoke with authority, commanding and demanding, directing the sale of evil and the exploitation of despair.

"Oh, shit," the girl's voice gasped in surprise.

"Yeah, that's right," the thickly-accented voice of his lead captor snapped. "Never thought you'd run into me again, did ya?"

"Oh," the darker voice, the one tugging at the edge of his memories, seemed to almost vibrate in anticipation. "I was hoping."

"Don't even try it, *puto*!" the tiny voice barked. From the stumble, he could sense the leader of his captors pull back, away from the new arrivals. "What are you fools waiting for? Drawn down!"

There was a rustle of clothes and the smell of gun oil. The two new arrivals were very still, though the lighter one, the girl, moved closer to the larger, heavier male. The tiny leader of his captors circled the room, away from the closet door, staying far from the new arrivals. "You two must be the dumbest motherfuckers in history!" the leader mocked, sitting at the far end of the room. "You really think you're just gonna walk into my place of business?"

"To be fair," the girl offered, "We didn't know you worked here."

"I don't work here!" the little leader barked, slamming a hand on a desk. "This is my place! My business! After all you fuckers done to me, I got mine back!"

"Not from Junior," the large male said, his voice staying even, and carrying the hint of threat, even in the simplest of words.

"No," the tiny leader agreed. "You made sure Junior wasn't takin' my calls. But somebody did. I found somebody who knows skill when they see it. Somebody fronted me enough to get this started. Junior won't have shit on me, soon. I'll be runnin' shit, and he can go fuck off to Telford with his *padre*. 'Course, that still leaves what I'm gonna do with you two."

"Two ways this can go, Juan," the menacing voice said flatly. "We're here for the boy you took from the *Drest-Vidar*. They had him. Now you have him. We're taking him. We can do this her way," he paused, and seemed to motion towards the girl next to him, "and everybody comes out of this in the same number of pieces." His voice, if possible, dropped even lower, carried even more menace and a terrible hunger for violence. "Or we can do this my way."

The tiny leader laughed, though his voice trembled with the memory of pain and humiliation. "Oh, fuck, that's good!" He was obviously forcing a bravado into a voice whose soul did not feel. "You think I ain't heard? A pretty little white girl and her beefcake bodyguard tearin' apart all the *Drest-Vidar* houses? All their businesses? A couple of do-gooders in white leather coats kickin' in doors! Yeah, bitches, I heard. I heard you two *malditas idiotas* been lookin' for some boy. Why you think I let word get out he was here? Huh? It's called a trap fuckers! And here you are, walkin' right into it."

"This doesn't have to end like this," the girl said. There was a note of almost desperation in her voice. She was not afraid, he realized, not for herself. Something within the girl's words, her heartfelt empathy, reverberated within him. She was afraid for others, perhaps for the scavengers in that very room. The girl wanted them all to live, to survive and be freed from an imminent suffering. He understood this, understood her. After all, he had spent generations trying to help Humanity endure the hardships it seemed to intent on inflicting upon itself. Like him, the girl wanted these Humans to avoid suffering and, like him, something in her knew it was too late.

"Yeah," the tiny leader argued. "It does, bitch. This fucker scars me, cuts off my hand, losses me EVERYTHING! You two make me a joke! You two take everything from me! You bet your narrow ass it has to go down like this! After my people kill this *maldito diablo* you whored yourself to, then we're gonna take turns on you, *puta*!"

Noises came through the crack beneath the door. Angry, vicious sounds. Gunshots went off, and heavy objects impacted each other. Sharp sounds of bones breaking accompanied the wet tears of bodies being violated. Screams came. Men begging for help, from their associates and from a God they had abandoned long ago. There were more crashes, more screams, more impacts.

Then, a hand emerged from the shadows behind him. The Celestial trapped in the form of a boy started and turned, and recognized an old face. The familiar vibration became strong as the Daimon revealed himself, reaching out from the hidden compartment in the rear of the closet. "Shh!" he hissed, putting a finger to his lips. "While they're distracted, we've got to go!"

The Celestial stared for a moment at the Daimon called Coyote by the Humans who had lived for generations in this place. He glanced back towards the sounds of destruction. "He won't help you," Coyote objected in a hushed, urgent voice. "Not yet. He's drawing too much attention to himself. If you want to be safe, come with me."

The Celestial imprisoned in a boy's body glanced again back towards the sounds of destruction. These, more than the unfamiliar voice, made him realize it was Za'afiel. He had witnessed the Angle of Destruction's work many times. He recognized the signs, the sounds, the feelings of being so close to Humans subjected to Za'afiel's wrath. He also knew that the Fallen Angel of Destruction had tried, once before, to protect someone, and that Human had died terribly at Za'afiel's own hands.

The Celestial grabbed Coyote's outstretched hand, and they fled into the tunnel once used to ferry people away who were in search of a better life.

Adam breathed deeply, standing in the center of the destroyed office. Men, groaning or unconscious, lay scattered in bloody heaps among the broken furniture. New holes in the walls joined with old ones. The overturned desk had been broken, and the drugs and money that had sat upon it were now flung to the corners of the room. Adam himself was disheveled, though no more so than usual, his white leather coat rumpled and stained with new, close-range gunshots.

"Well," Holly said with a look of disappointment at her partner. "That was gratuitous." She stood in the center of the room, knowing by now to hold still and allow Adam to work around her. "Did you kill any?" she asked, absently brushing non-existent dust from her black turtleneck sweater.

"No," Adam grunted. He looked around, scratching at his unshaven face. "Pretty sure, anyway." A limp, wet chunk of meat fell to the floor, leaving a bloody streak down the side of the wall. "Maybe that guy," the warrior conceded.

"So," his diminutive partner said in an even voice that the warrior had learned meant another lecture was coming. "What part of 'undercover' do you not understand?" She tugged at the edge of her own long, white leather coat, the match in style and color, though certainly not size, to the one Adam wore.

"What part of guns pointing at you do you not understand?" the warrior countered.

"Was I in any real danger?"

Adam started to mumble something.

"Exactly," she interrupted, her voice assuming that of a teacher, lecturing to errant schoolboys. "None."

The warrior sighed and glanced around for something to beat his skull against.

Holly was inspecting the moaning, groaning, and often unmoving remains of Adam's most recent act of undercover work. "This, like all our recent attempts, was supposed to be just gathering information." Daintly, she used the very tips of her tiny fingers to pull aside the flaps of coats and shirts, to explore pockets. "But, once again," her voice became like cold acid, "you overacted."

"Guns," Adam grunted. "Pointing at you."

"Like the last time," Holly continued, overruling his objection with a disdainful sniff. "That one idiot in the last house who called me a… what was it?"

"Sweet-smelling pussy pie," the warrior growled, more than spoke. Even the memory raised his ire, his hunger to punish.

"And you put his face through a brick wall," she reminded, retrieving a small bundle of folded papers from one unconscious man. "And then you grabbed his friend and…" she rolled her large, dark eyes, "you… bent him."

"I straightened him back out again," Adam objected.

"Only after I told you to!" Holly snapped, standing. She walked up to him, staring daggers up at his rugged, unshaven face. "You have to learn the virtue of proportionate response." She held up her hands, drawing an invisible line between them just as she drew out the syllables as she spoke. "Por-portion-ate re-sponse. Someone insulting me does not require you to go all…" she waved her hand at the broken office and its broken inhabitants.

"They started it…" Adam tried to object.

Holly held up a hand, the dark yellow of her painted nails catching the flickering light of the overturned lamp in the corner. "Five times," she snapped. "Five times we've been supposed to just go in, get information, and leave the rest to the cops. And five times…" she gestured again around the disheveled room and the broken bodies.

"But they pulled guns on you!" the warrior objected once again, feeling as though his central point was being lost.

"Is that thing bulletproof or not?" she snapped, pointing at Adam's white leather coat. "Does it really matter how many times they shoot you?" A moan of pain and despair drew her attention to behind the overturned desk. She crossed the room to look.

"Yours isn't," Adam muttered, mostly to himself. Seeing the cracked desk was in her way, Adam grabbed the side of the large wood frame and absently tossed it aside, clearing the way.

"What did you do to him this time?" Holly asked, looking down at the barely-conscious Juan.

"Nothing permanent," Adam grumbled, reaching down for the tiny criminal.

"Easy!"

The warrior corrected the strength of his grab. He righted the nearby chair and put Juan into it. "Is he conscious?" Holly asked.

Juan screamed, his one remaining hand going to the section of his scalp now missing hair. "He is now," Adam replied.

Holly absently swatted her partner's shoulder as she stepped towards Juan. Even without the heavy, lifting boots she wore, the young woman was much taller than the would-be crimelord cringing away from her. She looked down on him with a mixture of pity and resignation, no doubt suspecting how the rest of the night would proceed. "You know how this is going to go, Juan," she warned.

"Piss off, bitch!" Juan then screamed and ducked as a heavy gloved fist flew past where his head had just been, impacting the wall behind with enough force to shatter the crumbling plaster.

Adam grabbed the criminal's throat and half-lifted him out of the chair. "Speak to her with respect." The sound he made was less words, less a voice, than it was a heavy rumble drawn from the pits of the Earth.

Holly swatted her partner again, silently mandating that he release the criminal.

Tears and snot ran into the two jagged scars that formed an X across Juan's face. Holly sighed again and shook her head. "Look," she said in a voice filled with weary impatience. "How many times has it been, Juan? How many times have we caught you and run through this exact scene? We all know how this will play out. I act nice, you try to be tough, and then he gets violent. Can we, just this once, skip the dumb shit? Just tell us where the boy is."

For a moment, just the briefest instant, Juan looked as though he would force them through the same charade through which they had played before. This shadow of resistance gave way, though, and the informant pointed to a closet at the back of the room. Holly looked and crossed to the closed door. Her breath came short and her small hand trembled, though Adam suspected he was the only one who noticed. Their search for the missing boy who had called her for help had been frustrating, one failed lead after another. In truth, this evening represented what was probably their last chance at finding the boy.

Holly grabbed the doorknob and turned, pulling open the closet. Adam waited as she looked inside, only to return with a dejected look on her pretty face. They stared at each other, and she softly shook her head, water forming in her large, dark eyes.

Juan gasped, a gargling sound coming from his throat as Adam's fist slowly closed around it. The warrior looked down at that waste of flesh, that pitiful excuse for a Human who could only be bound for one place upon death and Judgement. "Don't lie to her," again the sound was more a pronouncement, a condemnation, then words. He twisted Juan's head one painful way, then the other. "Where. Is. The. Boy?" Each word was met with a further closing of Adam's fist. He kept twisting Juan's head to the side, matching his own tilt of the head.

"Swear," Juan gargled, pointlessly beating on Adam's unwavering, immovable arm. "Should… be… in… there."

"Just let him go," Holly said in a hollow voice. She turned to leave as Juan fell to the floor. "It doesn't matter."

2

"What's with the notepad?" Isandro asked with a nod towards Holly.

Adam glanced and saw that she was, once again, lost in her notes. His tiny partner was flipping through the small pages while pacing in small circles and letting mumbled words tumble from her small lips. "Says it helps her think," Adam told the good cop. "She writes down everything, all our leads, evidence, everything we do. Likes the feel of it in her hands." He shrugged. "That's what she says, anyway."

"Well, it obviously works," Isandro noted, consulting his own notes. "Five major drug busts in just over a month. All of them former *Drest-Vidar* holdings trying to start up again." The good cop nodded at the group of young women, barely more than girls, dressed in rags and half-starved. "Not to mention that, with this group, you two have saved more than a hundred girls from being sold overseas."

Adam grunted. He and Isandro were standing in the center of Juan's former office, out of the way of most of the work going on, while still close enough for the lieutenant to maintain oversight of his most recent operation. The warrior was also keeping an eye on Holly after their most recent failure to find the boy who had asked her for help.

Isandro glanced from Adam to Holly, the two men watching for a moment as she continued her circular pacing and intense scrutiny of her notebook. "It's got to be a good feeling," the good cop offered, "knowing she's helped so many people."

"Not the right one," Adam replied, forcibly keeping the concern from his voice. "And we've run out of leads."

They were standing away from Holly, giving her space as she concentrated. Isandro's team had arrived soon after the fight had ended, their allies having learned by now to leave the violence to Adam and his tiny boss. The perimeter had been secured with uniformed patrolmen, detectives had sectioned off areas, and forensic experts had collected evidence. Isandro himself, in command of this new law enforcement unit, had supervised everything. He maintained overwatch while leaving his people to their jobs, trusting in their skill. "How much longer?" Adam asked.

Isandro nodded at his dedicated forensic team, who were collecting their tools. "They're about done," the recently-promoted lieutenant answered. Adam had noticed that, when off-duty, Isandro's voice tended to drift into his Hispanic heritage, sailing among smooth vowels and rolling consonants. This was especially pronounced whenever the well-toned cop encountered a female, any female, who did not wear a uniform. Now, though, he was an icon of professionalism.

One of his subordinates, a dark-skinned man whose badge indicated he was a sergeant, stuck his head in the room. "LT," he called in a deep voice. "Services are here."

Isandro grunted and nodded. "Let them through." He said this in almost a sigh.

"Problem?"

"Crime Victim Services," the good cop replied, jamming his hands in the pockets of his overcoat. The December nights were growing unseasonably cold. Central Texas had a winter, contrary to what those who did not live in the state thought, but it usually only struck after the New Year. This Winter, though, pressed in on them, fogging their breath and stabbing needles into exposed flesh. "They've been taking charge of the victims you and Holly have rescued. They're supposed to give them shelter and help them back to their families."

"Supposed to?" Adam asked, noticing the good cop's use of words.

"Yeah," Isandro muttered. "Supposed to." A light appeared in his eyes, and he glanced at his sergeant. "Isn't that soup kitchen nearby?" he asked.

The dark-skinned sergeant nodded. "*La Cocnia de Abuela,*" he confirmed in rough, unpracticed Spanish. "About three blocks down. A few of their people were wandering around the barricade, but they left."

"Send a uni down. See if *Abuela* can take in a few strays."

The sergeant nodded and left.

"Who's this grandmother?" Adam asked.

"Another do-gooder," the good cop answered with a grin. "Like you." He glanced at Adam. "Well," he corrected with a nod towards Holly, "like her, anyway. She runs that soup kitchen and shelter. She's got a few people working with her: child care, *pro bono* lawyers, even a few doctors for a free clinic."

"You think social services hasn't been taking care of the girls we pull out of these places?"

"Victim Services are supposed to answer to the on-site commander. Really, though, our beloved Chief has made them answer directly to the City Manager," Isandro almost spat. "Girls from money are sent home, after a generous campaign contribution."

Adam looked calmly, very calmly, towards the girls who had been kidnapped, starved, beaten, and violated. They shivered under the heavy wool blankets Isandro's people had provided. They held steaming cups in unsteady hands and their eyes were wide and hollow, empty pools reflecting a trauma that would need years to heal, if it ever did. "And the rest?" he asked in a voice devoid of mercy.

"I can never get a solid answer," Isandro muttered. "None of the girls are ever from Disanté, or even Meropis county. They're often from all over the state, far outside my jurisdiction. I've gotten promises they make their way home, and then told to stick to my duties."

"This City Manager keeps sounding like a problem that needs to be dealt with," Adam mused.

Isandro shook his head. The good cop was about to say something when a commotion drew their attention. Both men walked down the short hallway to the front door, where a herd of media were shining lights at the house and already inventing stories without bothering to first learn any facts. Some of the reporters shouted questions to anyone wearing a badge or city service uniform. Others made blind, incendiary accusations, clearly hoping to elicit a response. Isandro's team ignored them, stoically facing down the public scrutiny and maintaining a perimeter.

"New arrivals," one of his detectives called from just outside the door. He was nodding towards an arriving van, this one belonging to *The Daily Crier*, Disanté's local newspaper. The van opened and a team of photographers, reporters, and internet commentators poured out, along with two familiar faces who immediately waved to Adam.

"Keep 'em back with the others," Isandro ordered without a glance, turning back into the house.

"It's the Twins," the detective replied. In the weeks since Isandro's team had begun working with Adam and Holly, his sisters had become a fixture, a pair of heavenly bodies orbiting and forever trying to get closer.

"Keep 'em back with the others," Adam grunted, joining Isandro back in the darker safety of the drug house.

Isandro glanced at his irritable ally as they returned to Juan's former office. "Family problems?" he asked with the barest upturn of his full lips.

Adam grunted again. "They keep asking about Christmas," he growled. "Keep talking about wanting to do… something."

The good cop shook his head in mock sympathy. "It must be terrible having family who cares about you."

Adam was about to snarl an appropriate answer, laced with a few colorful insults, when a disturbance drew their attention back to the hall again. A large group of civilians had arrived and were being let into the police barricade. Specific people were granted access, and the handful who tried to blend in, to sneak through with the arrivals, were firmly ejected by Isandro's team. Shouts accompanied the new group, but not from those outside the barricade who might object to the special treatment of these people. Nearly all the objections came from the employees of Victim Services.

"This is unacceptable!" a middle-aged woman, portly and officious, came stomping up to Isandro and Adam. She was bundled in layers of thick fabric against the growing cold, looking much like an officious toad, ready to snatch up any unwary fly. "Lieutenant Isandro!" she croaked, "This is an outrage!"

"What is it this time, Ms. Sapo?" the good cop asked with a sigh. Since the arrival of Ms. Sapo and her entourage of bureaucrats, she had inserted herself into every element of police business. In theory, she had been meant only to take charge of the kidnapped girls, offer them comfort, and see to their needs. Instead, she had lorded over Isandro's team, nearly ignoring the victimized young women while claiming to be keeping a record of the incident and demanding to be included in everything.

"I am the head of Victim Services," Ms. Sapo said, not for the first time that evening. "The kidnapped women are my responsibility!" She was nearly hopping from one foot to the other in her authoritarian outrage.

"And?"

The officious official pointed her clipboard at the new arrivals. The new arrivals were speaking to the victims, offering them warm smiles and asking them gentle questions. "You will make those, those… *people* leave this area immediately!"

"You will?" Adam asked Isandro in mock surprise.

"I am in charge of those girls!" Ms. Sapo said again. "They will go where I tell them to go! Not to some down-and-out shelter!"

"Actually," Holly's voice cut in from behind Adam and Isandro. "Unless they're under arrest, they can go wherever they want." She walked up to stand between the two men, shielding her eyes against the glaring light of the media.

Adam glanced over at Isandro. "Are they under arrest?"

"Nope," the good cop replied.

"That doesn't matter!" Ms. Sapo insisted, almost quivering in her anger. "They have to come with me!"

"Actually," Holly corrected, "according to Chapter 56a of the Texas Criminal Code, all victims, especially those of sexual assault, have the right to designate their own victim services provider." Standing at the top of the small porch, Holly was still much shorter than the toad-like woman, yet still she somehow towered over the officious bureaucrat. "Additionally, like anyone, they have the right to an attorney." She nodded to a pair of women handing business cards to the kidnapped girls. "One of their own choosing."

Ms. Sapo scrunched her face, furious at Holly's interference, and the revelation of how powerless the city official was. The red-faced bureaucrat took a half-step forward, bulging out her throat and seeming as though she might let loose a venomous assault on the smaller woman. She stopped dead, though, her bulbous eyes going up to Adam and Isandro, who had also taken a step forward to stand behind Holly. The men said nothing, did nothing, their faces implacable, unwavering. Ms. Sapo reversed her half-step and nearly hopped back, away from the guardians standing sentinel over the young woman who had thwarted her. She turned to Isandro. "Your superiors will hear about this, *lieutenant*!" With that threat, Ms. Sapo waddled off, impotently watching as the kidnapped girls were taken into the custody of the local do-gooders and led down the street to the waiting shelter.

Holly glanced up. "I had this," she objected with an annoyed upturn of the corner of her small mouth.

"Yes, you did," Adam agreed.

Isandro glanced at Holly. "Did you really memorize the Criminal Code?"

"Not all of it," she shrugged.

A large woman, not of girth, but of muscle, arrived then. The local cops melted away from her, none of them needing a command to give way. The barricade tape was lifted over her tall head, the two nearby patrolmen needing to stand on their toes to accommodate, as the woman would not bend. In the shining lights of the media, the silver star in a wheel pinned to the lapel of her long coat gleamed. "What're the Rangers doing here?" Adam asked.

"Ah, shit," Isandro sighed and straightened, moving to intercept the new arrival. "Frankie, baby." His words and his hips adopted a somewhat forced swagger. "What're you-"

The taller, larger woman cut him off by the simple expedient of closing his lips with her fingers. She did not spare him even a glance, instead staring at Adam and Holly. "How many is this for you two?" she asked.

"Five," the warrior answered. He was once again surprised at how soft, how lyrical, the Ranger's voice was, a jolting contrast to her hard, unyielding body and attitude.

She looked around. "That boy you're looking for wasn't here?"

Adam shook his head.

Holly approached the Ranger, smiling sadly up at the towering representative of those legendary lawmen. "We looked through the house," she said in a voice softer than the Ranger's, and lacking it's unflinching certainty. "We found the girls, but not him."

The Ranger released Isandro and turned, looking down at Holly and easing her hard face into something approaching kindness. "I saw the social workers," she said gently. "That's a lot of girls you've helped tonight, to say nothing of the other four groups" She put a gloved hand on Holly's shoulder, sensing, nearly as clearly as did Adam, Holly's growing remorse at their ongoing failures.

"Not the one we're supposed to be helping," Holly argued.

The Ranger put her gloved hands on her gunbelt, exposing the massive revolver holstered at her hip. "I've put the word out to my people," she said. "If anything turns up, we'll let you know."

Holly forced a smile up at the much taller woman. "Thank you, Lieutenant Haymer."

Haymer allowed a grin to upturn one corner of her lip. "You can call me Frankie," she offered. Then, the Ranger glanced dismissively at Isandro and the grin vanished. "You call me Lieutenant," she commanded, pushing past him and walking into the drug house with Holly following behind. "Or Ma'am," she finished.

Adam and Isandro trailed behind the two domineering women. "I'm a lieutenant too," he grumbled under his breath.

"Need to speak a little louder," Adam suggested. "If you really want your balls back, that is."

"You're one to talk."

Holly and Haymer entered Junior's former office and spoke softly with each other while the men stood at the door. The much-shorter Holly led the comparative giant through several points in the room, consulting her notebook about evidence she had collected. Haymer occasionally corrected one of her diminutive student's assumptions or false-deductions. Finally, Holly flipped to an apparently random page in her small notebook, this one baring a sketched diagram of various rooms. She glanced at Adam. "I need your help."

The warrior immediately went to her side.

"This room's the wrong size," she declared.

"What?" Isandro asked in confusion.

Holly continued consulting her notepad. "This is one of those cookie-cutter designs. All four of the houses we've busted had this same floorplan."

"Half of Texas has these tract-houses," Haymer shrugged. "But the owners are always making changes."

Holly pointed to the far wall in which the closet was built. "That wall is too close."

Adam moved to the wall and looked, then glanced back at Holly. "The closet," she directed him. The warrior turned and stuck his head into the small closet, noticing in passing the bundle of blankets in one corner and the smell of a prisoner. "It was used as a cell," he told Holly. "Someone was held in here for at least a few days." He sniffed the air. "He was locked in here."

"Along that wall," Holly said, pointing to the side of the closet's door.

Adam looked. He held up a hand without looking and Holly pulled a small light from her yellow-dyed leather belt. She turned it on and handed it to her partner. The warrior crouched. "See there?" he asked, directing

Holly's eyes to the baseboard. A series of small scratches, old and barely visible, were embedded into the floor, having torn through the thick, cheap carpeting of the closet.

"A door?" she asked.

"Stand back," Adam grunted.

"Hold on," Haymer said, pulling out her phone. "I'll get a good forensics team-" Her words were cut off by the impact of fist into wood. "Why do I even bother with these two?" she sighed in exasperation.

"You get used to it," Isandro offered helpfully.

Adam pulled until the hidden door released and slid aside. Holly offered her light again, and the warrior stared into the darkened passage.

"What is it?" Isandro asked having moved to the door way to stand and look over Holly's head.

"Tunnel," Adam grunted. He knelt and put his fingers to the ground. Once again, he directed Holly's gaze. Within the layers of dust and dirt, there were disturbances. Two sets of footprints, one large, one small, reached into the darkness. "Recently used."

"He was here," Holly whispered. "But where does it go?"

"Probably to a nearby house," Isandro suggested. "This looks like a coyote tunnel. This house was probably used as a safehouse for illegals trying to get further north. If immigration tried to raid the place, they could use this tunnel to get away."

Haymer glanced at him. "How do you know so much about smuggling illegals?"

"I'm a Texas cop in spitting distance of the border."

Adam handed the light to Holly and entered the tunnel with his partner directly behind and illuminating the path. "Wait!" Haymer tried to call, cutting her words off when their futility dawned on her.

"I'll have uniforms outside the neighboring houses!" Isandro called. "Give a yell wherever you come out!"

The tunnel dipped into the earth almost immediately. Steps had been carved into the stone, narrow and well-worn. Adam reached the bottom and turned back to offer a hand to Holly. This was likely unnecessary, since her tiny feet, even burdened with heavy, platformed leather boots, more easily accommodated the small steps than did Adam's overly-large gait.

"There're lights," Holly noted, pointing to the string of old lanterns strung along the tunnel.

"Used to be," Adam grunted, seeing lack of fuel or electrical cabling.

The tunnel was old and dying. The timbers holding the walls and ceiling were rotting. In two places, these had given way, and allowed the earth to half-fill the narrow passage. Although Holly had no difficulty in moving through these partial-collapses, Adam's hulking frame lost a fair amount of skin as he forced his way through. "Must be nice being small," he growled between curses.

"Try dieting," she said primly, absently brushing off some errant dust from her black turtleneck and straightening her own white leather coat.

The tunnel soon reached another set of old steps. Adam wordlessly gestured to Holly, who extinguished the small light. She stepped back and retrieved her pistol from its holster at the small of her back while Adam slowly climbed the steps. The warrior continued up into another closet, identical to the first but lacking the blankets and the stench of imprisonment. It's door was open and the house beyond was dark and still.

Adam leaned against the closet doorframe and glanced around. He reached out with all his senses, but found nothing. There was no furniture, no décor, no signs of any inhabitation. The windows were boarded up, and through them Adam saw the flashing lights of the police vehicles down the road. "Clear," he said without looking.

Holly entered and exchanged her pistol for her light. She shone it on the floor. "There," she said.

Adam looked and spotted the footprints, one large, the other small, moving from the closet to the front door. They paused in their escape at a small table. On this was a single piece of paper, folded and waiting. Adam picked up the paper and read it aloud. "You're drawing too much attention."

He handed the paper to Holly, who snatched it. She held her light close to it, examining the potential clue. "What's this?" she asked, staring at the engraved design in the bottom corner of the paper.

"It's a coyote."

3

"I'm sorry, Holly," Harun said with a gentle hand on the girl's shoulder.

"We've tried all our resources," Marun agreed, her arms crossed and a grimace on her face.

After leaving the abandoned house, Adam and Holly had walked back up the street. Isandro and Haymer had joined them with the Twins at their news van while their reporters continued inventing facts about the night's events. Holly had said nothing since finding the note, and Adam was at a loss of how to cushion this latest failure.

"Is there any sign of Kiliahoté?" Adam asked.

"Kiliahoté?" Haymer asked, her arms crossed over her large chest.

"A local museum curator," Isandro offered. The two stood close to each other, but with a noticeable separation.

"What's he got to do with any of this?" the Ranger asked.

"He's got something to do with everything," Adam grumbled. "He's been sticking his nose in my business since I got here."

"He's not at his house," Harun said, her arm still around Holly and her cheek resting against the much shorter girl's head.

"Or the Fort Burleson Museum," Marun added. "He hasn't been there in the last week or so. There's a notification that the museum will be closed over the holidays.

"Where is he?" Adam growled, mostly to himself.

"What's so important about some museum worker?" Haymer demanded.

"He's a Daimon," Adam almost spat. "The worst of them."

"Hardly the worst, big brother," Marun objected. She adjusted the collar of her yellow winter coat against the frosty wind.

"Just the most annoying," Harun added, pulling her red scarf free and wrapping it around Holly who was gently shivering even under her long white leather coat.

"To you, anyway."

"Are you following any of this?" Haymer demanded of Isandro.

"Hmm?" The good cop glanced at her. "I stop listening when they start in on all the woo-woo stuff."

"Probably best for you," Adam grunted.

"Humans don't usually do well around the 'woo-woo' stuff," Marun agreed.

"Not without our help at least," Harun added. She glanced at Adam. "You know, if he doesn't want you to find him, big brother, you won't."

Adam grunted his sullen agreement.

"He's that good at hiding?" Haymer asked.

Adam grunted again.

"What do we do now?" Holly asked in a voice barely above a whisper.

All eyes turned to her.

"We keep looking," Adam said with stony resolution.

"But, we've run out of leads," his partner objected.

"There's always something," Haymer told her. "There's always a clue you missed, a witness you can talk to, some evidence just waiting. You need to have faith."

Holly's hand went to the golden cross pinned to the collar around her neck. "Faith," she whispered, half to herself.

"And in the meantime…" Marun said.

"We've got some holidays to celebrate," Harun added. She looked at Adam with wide, manipulative eyes shining with insincere tears. "Right, big brother?"

Adam made a sound that was something between a grunt and a growl.

Isandro straightened. "Well, in the meantime, I've got this scene to process and a bunch of new scumbags to settle into jail."

"I've got to get moving, as well," Haymer noted with a glance at the time. "I'll need to talk to those survivors you rescued, then I'm off to El Paso for a few days."

"New case?" Isandro asked.

"All these girls the dynamic duo over here have rescued keep talking about the same trafficking network. I was hoping with the end of the *Drest-Vidar*, we would've seen the last of that for a while, but somebody's taken over the business. I've had more than enough of that shit, so I'm heading to the source.

"Juarez?" Isandro guessed.

"Maybe," Haymer shrugged. "If I need to." The tall Ranger walked over to Holly and put a hand on her shoulder. "In the meantime, keep the faith."

Holly looked up and nodded.

The tall Ranger nodded back with a half-smile, then she turned and left.

"Really?" Adam grunted at Isandro's gaze as it lingered over Haymer's departure, his eyes especially lingering on specific parts of her.

"What can I say?" the good cop almost sighed. "I've got a type."

"Yeah, breathing." Adam looked at Holly. "There's not much else to do here," he said, trying to ease some of the irritation from his voice.

She nodded.

"We'll pick this up after some sleep. Put fresh eyes on it in the morning."

"Actually, big brother," Harun objected, her arm still around Holly. "You have other plans."

Marun stepped beside Adam with a grin. "That's right. Didn't you promise to take a certain lady to the tree lighting tomorrow?"

Adam growled something inarticulate at each of the Twins in turn. Then, an idea presented itself. "The kid's more important," he insisted. "We can't give up the trail."

"No," Holly objected. "Candice has been looking forward to this for weeks." She looked up at Adam. "Will Kiliahoté hurt the boy?"

"Probably not," the warrior conceded.

"Actually," Harun added, "of all the Daimons, Coyote has always been the most helpful to Humans."

"Or means to be, anyway," Marun agreed.

"He usually has good intentions."

"And tries his best to do what he thinks is best for you."

"Long as it's funny," Adam grumbled.

"Don't be such a… you," Marun said, swatting his shoulder.

"He's just… mischievous," Harun agreed.

"So he's trying to help the little boy?" Holly asked.

"Probably."

The tiny girl straightened then and looked at Adam. The warrior recognized that look and sighed, realizing that imperious proclamations were forthcoming. "Then you're going on that date," she declared.

"Candice has already picked out the best clothes for tomorrow," Harun agreed.

"With some help from us, of course," Marun added.

"It's important to her," Holly decreed, "and you're not going to ruin it for her."

"Like usual," the Twins said in unison.

Adam was about to argue, to assert his right to self-determination, a right forced upon him by the Choir after his Fall. Any objections, though, any claims of Free Will, died on his lips. Standing in the street, righteous heat was pouring from three set of feminine, tyrannical eyes, forcing away the sullen winter. So, the warrior only sighed, his shoulders slumping against the pressure of authoritarian women.

4

The ride to Candice's house was quiet. Conversation was always challenging with the Beast's roaring engine, but Holly always found a way. Most recently, she had installed some bizarre communications system into their helmets, so that she could continue issuing orders to her sullen slave, even as they rode. Over the past months of their collaboration, Adam had grown somewhat used to the incessant buzz of her words. Whenever the two went from one place to another, the warrior let his partner's unending tide of conversation blend into the background hum of the world. The Beast's engine, the clawing of his wheels upon the road, birds nearby and far, traffic and urban suffering, all blending together with Holly's unending observations and opinions. But that morning, the young woman was silent.

Candice's house was in one of the many small neighborhoods scattered at the edges of Disanté. Adam and Holly had needed to ride alongside the far edge of Fort Burleson, the small road tracing a path along the edge of the airfield shared by both the Army and the civilian airport. With the holiday season in full force, there were no helicopters in the air, no roar of rotors or propellers and surprisingly-few civilian planes. The base was still and the airport sleepy, their aircraft sleeping away until the new year arrived. They passed the last of the convenience stores, short-term loan and pawn shops, car dealerships, and other hallmarks of modern civilization, cutting uncomfortably deeper into the suburban wilderness and its own particular dangers.

The Beast seemed as agitated as the warrior who rode him. *He must be sensing Holly's distress*, Adam mused as they rode. They were much alike, the warrior realized. He had been an Angel of Destruction, the raging punishment upon Humans whenever they evoked Celestial wrath. But now he was Adam Kadmon, a man. All of his countless centuries of experience, of violent capability and skill, imprisoned within hard, unyielding meat. So it was with the Beast. Once a proud spirit of the untamed jungle, he had been forced into this motorcycle form. Whenever Adam grasped the high-angled, low-swept handlebars, he felt the agitated impatience of the Beast. Whenever they rode upon the ugly black Human roads, the rider felt his mount's desire for a jungle floor vibrating up through the front suspension, now twisted into a mockery of the Beast's former feline forelegs and claws. The low, rigid saddle was a poor replacement for the spirit's former back, once supple and graceful. The yellow, stylized headlights always seemed to narrow in memory of the Beast's former predatory cat-eyes. Yes, they were much alike in their physical prisons, and during their rides the two, rider and bike, shared in their own discomfort with their sensing of Holly's disquiet.

As they turned onto Candice's street, the Beast once more grumbled his concern. The bike's discontent was not directed towards their destination. In fact, in the times Adam had spent with Candice, the Beast seemed nearly as fond of her as he was of Holly. Whenever the bartender rode with them, the bike took obvious efforts to smooth their trip, just as he did when the burgeoning detective rode. The Beast extended his tires and shock absorbers to offer both women a smoother ride. He extended his passenger seat's back to offer the women better support. The Beast showed Holly obvious preference and deference, purring contentedly in her presence and being overly-protective of the younger woman. Still, Candace had become a seemingly welcome inclusion into the otherwise torturous life of this misshapen creature.

They pulled into the driveway of Candice's small house close to noon. The tree lighting in town would not happen until after sundown, but Holly had been insistent that Adam take her to Candice's house early. Like so many in Central Texas, the home had only a single floor. There were no trees or shrubbery in the front yard, instead having some well-manicured, low grass. A garage was attached to the house, and the small approaching walkway twisted around this to the front door. Twinkling lights glittered in the dim light of dusk, blinking a merry welcome to the winter holiday. A plastic replica of Saint Nicholas stood in the company of what appeared to be a plastic woman; this would be Mrs. Claus, Adam guessed, though he knew for a fact that the real Nicholas had never married. Across from the jovial plastic couple, on the other side of the short walkway leading to the front door, was another plastic couple: a snowman and his apparent wife. These two pairs of romantic partners seemed to be waving at Adam, encouraging him to approach.

Holly dismounted as silently has she had ridden, hefting the large bag strapped to her back. She pulled off her helmet, letting the cold wind caress her flowing black mane. She had changed its color again, replacing the previous blue highlights with a single golden streak on one side.

"You're not riding with us?" Adam asked, taking her helmet.

"The Twins are coming," Holly answered, her voice showing and obvious effort at sounding indifferent. She patted the Beast's passenger seat. "There's only room for two." She then took a step back and made to turn. "Now go bathe," she commanded her surly companion. "Him too," she said with a dismissive wave towards Adam.

The warrior, uncertain as ever when he was forced outside his expertise of violence, reached out a hand and caught Holly's. "The kid's alive," Adam said. "And you haven't given up."

The burgeoning detective stiffened just slightly, but did not pull her hand away. "It doesn't change that he asked for help," she said in a soft voice, her large, dark eyes turned away. "It doesn't change that I-"

"You didn't fail," Adam interrupted, knowing full well the feelings twisting her young soul. He knew, because he knew what it was to have someone ask for help, and fail them. "And you haven't given up."

Holly looked out, past Fort Burleson's air field, into the urban blight called Disanté. "He's out there," she almost whispered. "And I'm going to a Christmas party."

Adam took her tiny chin in his large fingers, turning her gaze to his with the lightest possible touch. "Yeah, he's out there," the warrior confirmed. "He's alive and he's safe. And you're exhausted."

"I'm fine-" she was about to lie.

"We live in the same apartment, remember?" Adam pointed out. "I know you aren't sleeping. I've seen your conspiracy board in the bedroom. I've heard you muttering through the night. I know what it feels like to-" his words cut off, the memory of failure threatening once more to crash against his unwanted soul.

"You never talk about it," Holly pointed out, looked up at her partner. Even with her standing and he seated in the Beast's saddle, still he was taller than her. "Maybe you should."

"We're talking about you," Adam deflected. "You're worn out. You need a night away from it. Relax, enjoy the Winter Solstice."

"Christmas," she corrected.

"Whichever." The warrior waved away the distinction. "You people change your holidays too damn often."

"It's been, like, two thousand years," Holly pointed out.

He held up a finger. "Remember, this was your idea. If you're going to force fun on me, then you've got to do it too. We'll take tonight for this nonsense, then get back at it in the morning, fresh."

"But-"

"No buts. We take the night. Tomorrow, we find the boy. That's how it is."

The Beast pressed his forward wheel against Holly's leg and hip, his engine purring in concern. Holly smiled and rubbed a hand on his suspension. "Go clean up," she commanded again. "Have him back at four."

With that, Holly had turned and walked to the front door, being admitted with the portal closing behind her firmly. Adam and the Beast had remained for a moment in the driveway. Beneath the surely warrior, the Beast grumbled another low objection. Adam, who had remined seated in the saddle, grimaced his agreement. "Yeah," he said, holding a lingering grip on the throttle. "I'd rather be riding too." His words came with a gaze to the horizon. Not for the first time, his mind wandered to the roads beyond Disanté and Meropis County, even beyond Central Texas. There were a great many open paths and free lands in this world, he knew. For all their belief of mastery, Humans still occupied very little of this garden, even as they tried so hard to poison it. Most of the Fallen became wanderers, drifting from place to place, limiting their exposure to Humans. The desire to be free from all this self-inflicted suffering was tempting.

"Why don't you go?" a smooth voice asked from behind.

Adam sighed. He had known Simkiel was there, of course. After all, he was always there. Even as stunted as the warrior's senses were, trapped in this Human body, he still knew when a Celestial was close. Angels could make themselves undetectable, but Simkiel rarely chose to do so. "Aren't you supposed to be watching?" he growled at his Watcher. "Not talking?"

Simkiel flowed around the Beast, careful to keep a safe distance. He always moved with smooth grace, Adam had noticed. Whether in his real, ethereal form, or the one he presented now. Celestials, when they appeared to Humans, chose their appearance. This form was a combination of the expectations of nearby people and the Angel's own nature. Adam, as Za'afiel, had always appeared as a warrior, a bringer of Destruction. Simkiel, though, was another matter, always appearing well-dressed and well-groomed, an icon of refined style and class. Thus, his current appearance was surprising to Adam.

"What in Hell happened to you?" the former Angel of Destruction almost laughed.

Simkiel's silk suit was rumpled and even torn in a few places. The Angel's normally-perfect hair, a full coif of flowing blonde, was nearly as unruly as Adam's, sticking out at odd angles and stiffly wilting as the Angel shook his head. "There've been a few… disagreements about how to proceed with what comes next," he said.

Adam took in the Angel's apparently-unshaven face and the heavy bags under his eyes. Celestials of all kinds did not need sleep any more than they needed food or drink. They did suffer from weariness, even exhaustion, though. "It looks like the disagreement has gotten intense," the warrior said without concern for his former brother.

"To put it mildly," Simkiel huffed. "The Chorus is of two minds whether or not to warn you."

"About…?"

Instead of offering an overt answer, Simkiel turned his gaze to the house and the women inside. The soft glow of his halo brightened slightly, granting Adam a portion of Celestial sight. Within the house, Holly and Candice were moving to a bathroom, chattering about love and sex and other foolish things. The two women were preparing to bathe and readying cosmetics and clothes as though they were readying for war.

"They're so vulnerable," Simkiel mused. "All Humans, really, but those two especially." They continued to look as Holly manipulated a shower, testing the water and beginning to remove her clothes. Adam reached out and forcefully moved Simkiel's head, averting his gaze. "Do you remember what I told you after you saved that girl from Paimon's cult?" the Angel asked.

"You made some veiled threats," Adam recounted. "You pointed out how many enemies I've made over the centuries and that, sooner or later, they'll come."

"Sooner, rather than later," Simkiel amended.

Adam narrowed his eyes. "So who is it?" he nearly growled. "Who's coming?"

"Here," the Angel corrected. "Not coming, here."

"Alright, who's here?"

Simkiel did not move, did not speak. The Angel did not change in the slightest in how he presented himself to Adam. Still, the warrior recognized when a Celestial was being forced to do something, or to not do something. Simkiel was trying to speak, and was being prevented.

"They won't let you," Adam guessed. "'Watchers, not Talkers.' That's what Samyaza always said." Adam's face twisted into a knowing, dark grin. "Until he Fell, of course."

"You have Free Will now," Simkiel reminded the Fallen, a brief shadow falling over his face at the mention of his former commander. "You choose and you must live with your choice."

Adam put his hands on the Beast's handlebars and straightened, both imprisoned warriors ready for the confrontation to be at an end. "Well, I choose for you to piss off."

"You can still leave," Simkiel managed to say, obviously working around the limitations imposed upon him by the Chorus. The Angel nodded to the horizon. "You can go, and take what's coming with you." He then looked again to the house, and to where Holly and Candice, both naked and exposed, were happily preparing for the night's celebration. "Or you can stay."

Then, the Angel was gone.

Adam and the Beast remained in the driveway for a while. He had made his choice weeks ago. After the defeat of the *Drest-Vidar*, Simkiel had given them the same choice. Rider and bike could leave, wander the open roads alone and be free of all this messy humanity. Or, they could stay, and be burdened by Holly and Candice and all the others. The Beast had deferred to Adam, and the warrior had chosen. But now, the possibility of danger was a reality. Any number of threats existed, once thwarted by Za'afiel and now eager for vengeance. Holly and Candice and the Twins and all the others would be caught up in what was to come. He could spare them that suffering; he probably should.

But he had given his word. Adam had promised her they would find the boy who had asked her for help. She was learning quickly the arts of tracking, of detecting and deducting. She had even asked Adam to teach her some basic hand-to-hand defense. Holly was learning quickly, but she was not yet ready to work alone. She probably could not find the boy on her own, not even with help from Isandro and Haymer. If Kiliahoté was involved, then her chances decreased from slim to almost none. Adam knew the Coyote; he understood how a Trickster operated. If they left, his promise to Holly would be broken.

So, Adam did not have to choose, but rather only reaffirm the choice already made.

Four hours later, having obeyed Holly's commands, Adam and the Beast returned to Candice's house. The warrior grumbled as he dismounted, retrieving the bouquet he had sullenly purchased. Once more, he grimaced at the pungent odor coming off the dying plants. The florist had called this a winter bouquet, and Adam's eyes watered at the bewildering riot of colors. Red and white roses were mixed with something the merchant had called candy cane lilies. She had insisted that Candice would love them, and that they smelled "just divine." To the warrior, they only smelled like overpriced weeds.

Outside Candice's house waited the Twin's luxury pickup truck. Adam rolled his eyes with a shake of his head, noticing that they had, once again, had the vehicle painted. Hardly a month seemed to pass without the Twins modifying that poor truck. They had it lowered, then lifted. They had a new sound system installed, then upgraded. New tires. A new exhaust. New interior lighting. A new bed liner. New running boards. New. New. New. Now, they had again repainted it, with multitone yellow and highlights of blue and red. The Beast grumbled at the obvious attention the Twins paid to their truck. "Forget it," Adam growled.

The warrior sighed and rubbed again at his face. He hated the feeling of shaving. His skin felt as though it had been peeled and every errant breath of cold winter air pushed mockingly against his jaw. The warrior could not stand the feeling of having the familiarity of himself scraped away, of having the rawness beneath exposed for any casual viewer. Holly had insisted though, demanding, berating, insulting, and cajoling him into obeying her specific instructions. He had washed, shaved, and applied some idiotic perfume the tiny tyrant had insisted would make him "smell like a man." She had forced him to wear the new pants and shirt she had purchased, with his money. Much like shaving, Adam hated new clothes.

The jeans were unbroken, unyielding, and uncomfortable. The new brown belt matched the new boots, both tan leather in need of far more weathering. Even the dark red shirt was fuzzy and itchy, scratching against the muscles of his chest and arms whenever the warrior moved. The only concession Adam had won was his long white leather coat.

Adam uncomfortably stood before Candice's front door wishing for a battlefield or a natural disaster or some other welcome relief, but was granted none. He stabbed the doorbell with an irritated knuckle and glanced again skywards. He could almost hear the laughter echoing from the Silver City.

"It's about time," Holly snapped as she opened the door.

"What?" Adam blinked, surprised and unsurprised in the same moment. He glanced back at the fading sun. "I'm on time."

"You're not early enough," she sniffed, inspecting him closely. Holly then sighed and shook her small head. "Good enough, I guess."

His tiny partner was already dressed for the tree-lighting. She was wearing a knitted skirt and sweater of pale blue, with frilly white lace at the hem and cuffs. She had white leggings to shield from the biting breeze outside and as always wore her thick-soled leather boots. Her cross rested against a lace collar and matched the other simple jewelry adorning her fingers and ears. Her long, dark hair flowed freely down her head, though the yellow streak had been arranged into a braid. This mane probably helped to insulate her neck and shoulders against the winter, Adam surmised. She turned and irritably gestured for her servant to enter. The warrior shook his head and obeyed, closing the door behind. "She's still getting ready," Holly declared, walking down the short hallway into the living room. She paused and glanced back, noting the flowers in Adam's hand. Holly nodded slightly.

Inside the short hall, Adam spotted a line of graceful hooks. Upon one was Holly's white leather coat, the match of Adam's and unmistakable for how small it was. Upon two more were a pair of nearly-identical cashmere coats with fur linings, one blue and the other yellow. A fourth coat, Adam guessed, was Candace's. Simple and warm red plaid with a fur-lined hood. The warrior paused at the line of coats and glanced down; a high bench rested below the coats, holding keys, purses and some of the various other additions these modern Humans always seemed to need whenever they left their homes. Among these, sitting exactly beneath Candace's coat, was a new motorcycle helmet. Adam blinked and stared, needing a moment to realize what he was looking at. It was in the exact same style and design as Adam's. Holly had presented his new helmet in the days after their battle against the *Drest-Vidar*. Oddly, it did not match hers as had the previous ones. Instead, Holly had gotten for herself some bubblegum nightmare of a helmet, with an eye-watering design of red, blue, and gold flowering vines all intertwined with each other. Adam's unwanted helmet was a simple black with red highlights, though close inspection revealed some bizarre patterning within the black, but nothing too outlandish. Adam had been so relieved to be spared Holly's typical urge towards unnecessary adornment he had made only a few, perfunctory complaints. Now, he realized the truth.

The new helmet, obviously meant for Candace, matched Adam's perfectly. It was of the same design physically, and it had the same color scheme, but reversed: red with black highlights. Additionally, the strange patterns on Adam's helmet were present upon Candace's in every detail. Even the pentacle in white on the back was the same. Adam picked up the helmet and examined it, his eyes narrowing in suspicion of conspiracy. This growing paranoia was proven correct when he looked up and noticed that the red plaid of his new shirt matched perfectly Candace's coat. He held an arm up to compare the two garments and then narrowed his eyes at Holly.

Adam continued deeper into Candace's lair, glancing into the kitchen as he passed. It was larger than he expected, and well-appointed. Copper pots hung from traditional mountings near the stove. A variety of utensils, most of which the warrior could not identify, were neatly arranged on the countertops, along with glass jars containing various compounds. A long string of dried orange slices were hung like garland along the walls of the kitchen, filling the air with a citrus tang. Small artificial snowflakes hung from the overhead light, glittering merrily. A small dining table sat against one wall and, upon this, was a natural log. Into this had been carved holes into which Candace had apparently placed votive candles. The log was further surrounded by flowering holly and evergreen branches. An inviting warmth radiated from the kitchen, tempting Adam with glad tidings of comfort and… something more.

The warrior shook off the kitchen's siren call and continued into the living room. Just before, there was an opening in the hallway opposite the kitchen, leading to another short hall with two rooms and a guest bathroom. One of the guest bedrooms was open, and Adam could see it had been set up with a work table and all manner of fabrics as well as arts and craft supplies. The door to the other guest room was firmly closed, and, even without his Celestial senses, Adam could feel a wall of sorrow behind that sealed portal.

The warrior shook off the horrid memory of old pain coming from that closed room and entered the living room. He absently ducked under the hanging mistletoe and looked around. Like much of the house he had seen, this room had wood floors. The furniture was simple, but looked comfortable. Wood frames held brightly-colored cushions, each with a variety of holiday-themed decorations from carols to cartoonish Christmas characters. A fireplace rested against one wall, but had no fire. Instead, a log rested in front as though awaiting the coming holiday. Evergreen boughs had been tied upon the patient wood, and three unused red candles stood atop it. The log had been further decorated with pinecones, holly, and dried orange slices. Natural garland hung from the ceiling line, and tiny white lights had been strung within that, twinkling as though in counter-harmony to the emerging stars outside. A glass door rested opposite where Adam had entered, through which the warrior could see the back yard and its well-maintained, hibernating garden. This was, he realized, not a house, but rather a true home.

"Sit," Holly commanded as she walked across the living room to an open door beyond. "She's almost ready."

The tiny tyrant disappeared through the door. Looking, Adam saw this was the master, or rather mistress, bedroom. The typical accoutrements were there: dressers of various shapes and sizes. A large bed dominated the room's center with a great, heavy blanket offering shelter and comfort against the worsening winter outside. A pair of nightstands stood on either side of the bed, though the lamps that would normally be on these had apparently been replaced with, as yet unlit, candles. There was another small table, off to the side of the room, that was distinctly separated from the others. This was covered in a rich black fabric that caught the fading light in iridescent sparkles, and upon it were resting a small knife, a cup of water, a pentacle medallion, a crystal rod, and a small statue of a nude woman. Another statue that matched the first in size and design, but his one of a veiled woman, rested on a nightstand, away from the table. A strange scent filled the air of the room, one Adam could not place but stirred a strange feeling deep within him. The entire room had been recently, and thoroughly, cleaned. None of this held Adam's attention, though. Instead what fixated him was a painting above the bed. It was of a woman, perhaps some goddess or heroine, wrapped in a gold robe and kneeling upon jagged rocks. She was pale, and her hair was stylized into shafts of wheat. Small red flowers seemed to be falling from her to die upon the rocks as the world behind her withered. It was a sad painting, an image of sorrow and loss, out of place within a room that had been made warm and inviting.

"Wait in the living room," Holly commanded as she proceeded into to the mistress bathroom, firmly closing the door behind her.

Adam could hear a great chattering of female voices from behind that door and one again considered the open road. He sat on the large couch in the living room and waited.

And waited.

And waited.

The outside light continued to dim as time passed. The feminine chattering continued, occasionally accompanied with cackling laughter, some sounding faintly raunchy. The warrior could do nothing, though. He was used to patience. Many were the times in which he had to hold his position over some city or village. Oftentimes, the Chorus had sent him to wait above an army or town, allowing the Humans one last chance to avoid destruction. They rarely did, though. So Adam was accustomed to waiting. He waited.

And waited.

And waited.

Finally, after some interminable span of ages, the bathroom door opened once more. Holly emerged, followed by the Twins. They wore nearly-identical outfits to one another, both in pristine white dresses that reached the calves. Both had their hair unbound, flowing around their shoulders and down to the small of their backs. Where they differed was in the sweaters each wore. They were of identical material, but as usual, Harun wore blue while Marun wore yellow.

The three women passed Adam by with smirks and some barely-suppressed giggling. Marun paused to pin a small sprig of evergreen on Adam's shirt. "Say something nice to her," she whispered.

Harun made a passing attempt to straighten Adam's disheveled hair. "Or at least not stupid," she added.

"We're going on ahead," Holly said as she retrieved her white leather coat from the hallway. The Twins retrieved their own coats and the three women departed.

A cleared throat tried to draw Adam's attention back to the bedroom, but what first tugged at his senses was not the sound, but rather the scent. A delicate fragrance drifted through the air. It daintily brushed against Adam, teasing against his nostrils and seeming to slip into his lungs of its own accord. The warrior breathed deep, his eyes half-closing before he was aware of the acts. He glanced and stared.

Candace wore knee-length swede boots, the color the same as Adam's own rough footwear. Black pants clung to her legs and hips, perfectly emphasizing the generous curves and lines of her body. A knitted red sweater, similar in color to Adam's shirt but a few shades brighter, enveloped her torso, but did nothing to hide the generous swell of her breasts. Instead, the pattern on the sweater seemed somehow to highlight the rise and fall, each breath an inviting gesture. Her long auburn hair crowned her head and framed her face, glowing in the faint light of the twinkling garland overhead. Brightest of all was her smile, warm and red, parted slightly as one breath after another caught at Adam and drew him in.

The warrior did not remember standing, nor moving to her. He was only aware of suddenly standing before her. Heat radiated from the flush of Candice's cheeks and her large eyes held his own dull orbs. "Hi," he said.

She breathed deeply again, her smile even brighter in its proximity. "Hi yourself," she said. The bartender glanced down, her eyes tracing along Adam's body before lighting on what was in his hands. "Are those for me?" she asked.

"Flowers," he identified, handing the bouquet to her.

Candace smiled again, her tongue lighting just slightly along her upper lip. "Why, thank you. It's always nice when a gentleman caller brings flowers."

"Holly told me to," he said for some reason.

"Still," she said with a hand resting against his strong heart. "It's very considerate of you."

Once more unsure of how or why the motion started, Adam leaned forward just slightly, into Candace's touch. "What do we do now?" he asked, genuinely unsure.

Candace's smile darkened just slightly, though not from anger or weariness, but as though from some inner conversation. "Oh," she nearly purred, "I have a few ideas."

5

The air was cold. It was not the chill of weather, but rather the anticipation of it. Heavy clouds were overhead, and each gust of wind brought with it a promise of what was to come. These were not forceful, nor even baleful thrusts of air; instead, the erratic breeze brushed against them, sliding amidst the celebrants. Adm could taste the moisture on this subtle wind; he could feel the pressure building. Central Texas, contrary to what many thought, did get its share of winter weather. This was not, though, a steady blanket, but rather sporadic, furious storms. The solstice was nearly upon them, and Winter, it seemed, was building Herself in anticipation of it.

In response to Winter's encroachment, the people of Disanté raised their spirits even higher. Tall heating units were spaced across the great lawn in front of the new City Hall, but these were nearly redundant. Friends, families, and lovers wandered together, basking in a fellowship that forced away, however briefly, the gathering storm. The surrounding shrubbery twinkled with artificial constellations, blending their light with the multi-colored strings that had been gathered between the various lightposts like a merry spider's web. In each of the windows of the grand building from which city government ruled was centered a wreath, glowing and festooned with red ribbons.

"Is it always this… cheery?" Adam grumbled as he took Candice's new helmet and deposited it one of the Beast's saddlebags. The flashing lights from an engine of the Disanté Fire Department were stabbing into the warrior's eyes as though trying to grab and hold his attention. The Beast also growled his displeasure, the imprisoned spirt preferring the natural light of the forest.

"No," Candice smiled. The bartender glanced at where the local Santa Claus, having been recently delivered by the fire truck, cheerfully greeted giddy children. "In fact, the tree-lightin' is usually pretty tame. No decorations or music. It's usually just local officials and some business leaders. This is the first time I've come in years." Adam finished putting his own unwanted and unnecessary helmet in the bag and turned to face her. "It's almost like somethin's changed," she said softly, looking into his eyes.

Adam shrugged and looked around. "So," he said somewhat lost, "what do we do?"

"The lightin' isn't for a little while yet," she answered. "We look around."

The warrior nodded and fell in beside Candice. As they walked, their hands drifted together. Adam was unsure if he reached out to her, or if she reached out to him. Their bodies seemed, somehow, to move towards one another, unseen and unknowable currents making subtle alterations to their course. Together, they began wandering.

Many booths had been set up in orderly rows. These offered a plethora of items from toys and candy to clothes and jewelry. Everything was handmade and sold by local artisans. "Reminds me of the way things were," Adam noted as they approached a booth offering various soaps, balms, and oils.

"What do you mean?" Candice asked, sniffing at various bars of soap.

"This is how Humans have always done business," Adam shrugged. "Before you industrialized, anyway. It was always small markets, local merchants."

Candice held a bar to Adam's nose. "What do you think?" she asked.

The warrior breathed in. "Uh, flowery?"

"It's jasmine." She gently rubbed the bar against her wrist, and then waved that beneath Adam's nose. "How about now?" she asked.

Adam paused. Something had caused his brain to skip a beat. "What?"

Candice smiled and handed the bar of soap to the merchant. "I'll take it."

The vendor, an older woman smiling in nearly the same way as the bartender, put the soap in a small paper bag and handed it back to Candice. "I'll get that," he said as the merchant awaited her payment.

"Oh, you don't have to," Candice objected, though not making any move for her wallet, which Adam then realized, she was not carrying.

The warrior paid and they continued. When they passed a food vendor, he noticed Candice breathe deeply the scent of warm cider, so he purchased two cups of the steaming beverage, handing one to her. The bartender took the drink, letting her hand drift on Adam's. "Would you like me to hold that?" he asked, indicating the small bag.

"Oh, you don't have to," she objected as she handed it over.

"It's no problem." The warrior took the bag and rolled it around the small bar of soap, storing it in the side pocket of his white leather coat.

The pair wandered through the market, Candice often stopping to look at the various vendor's wares. She lingered in the booth of a local woodcarver, her eyes lingering over several smaller pieces. "It feels like we should be talking about something," he noted while the bartender traced her fingertips over a small carving of a black bear.

"That's usually how this works," she replied softly, her touch tracing along the bear. The image had been sanded and polished so that it looked nearly as smooth as glass. The woodcarver had also been meticulous with the stain, so that the carving had layers of coloring, truly replicating the look of a black bear.

"What do people usually talk about?" Adam asked, standing just behind Candice, not touching, but very close.

She leaned back slightly closing nearly all of the distance between them. "Oh, little things, at first. Favorite food, and favorite music. Some personal history, if they want."

As she stepped out of the woodcarver's booth, Adam glanced back and accepted the business card the artisan offered. He checked to make sure the needed information was there before storing the card in his pocket and catching up to Candice. They continued through the market. Holiday music was playing from the stage at the entrance stairs of City Hall, but as they were at the far edge of the lawn, this was muted. As Adam and Candice made their way from booth to booth, the bartender often stopping to examine the various merchant's wares, this background din was gently replaced by another source. So soft, Adam at first did not hear and could not separate this other music from the recordings blaring out from the distant stage. As he and Candice drew closer, though, this other sound slowly overrode the commercial noise.

Sensing Adam's attention, Candice led them towards its source. In the place of a vendor's tent, a pair of musicians had set up chairs. The young men, little more than boys, really, were sitting and playing their instruments, one a cello and the other a violin. They harmonized perfectly, their music drifting through classical carols and hymns, and their faces lost within their art. A small crowd was gathered in front of the two boys, though few lingered for long. In front of the musicians were their instrument cases, and in this was a scattering of low-denomination bills and coins. Almost entranced, Adam stood before the boys as they played.

The musicians finished a traditional carol and looked up, seeking requests. "Do you know 'War Requiem,' by Britten?" Adam asked.

The boys did know it, taking up the work immediately and without needing to confer. This was not a holiday song, not in the way most people expect and demand, so the crowd dispersed. Adam stood as the boys led their instruments through the composition, not wanting to feel, to remember, but also unable to prevent the past from returning. The cold air of Central Texas became that of London, and of the woods beyond. The lawn of Disanté's City Hall became the rebuilt city and the uneven ground of the forest. The boys became their past counterparts, just as young, and just as talented. Only Candice remained, standing beside him, saying nothing.

When the music was finished, Adam reached into the side pocket of his white leather coat and deposited a large roll of high-denomination bills into one of the cases, and then an equal roll in the other. The warrior turned and walked away, not hearing the excited boys call out their gratitude and wishing him a Merry Christmas.

"So," Candice said gently, "you've got a taste for Classical?"

Adam grunted, almost silently.

"I'm more of a Shania Twain fan, myself," she admitted. "Though, I suppose every Texas girl listens to Shania."

Adam grunted gain as they continued wandering through the last of the booths.

"I can talk about the lights," Candice suggested, walking beside Adam. "If you prefer."

The warrior paused and finished his now-cold cider. Spotting a distant trash can, he crumpled the paper cup and tossed it with barely an aiming glance. "My last mission," he said then. "It's not something I… It's not a good story."

"I won't pry," she promised. "We can talk about other things." The bartender stopped him, then, with the gentlest of touches to his thick chest. "But I would like to know."

The warrior said nothing at first, letting the commercialized noise of popular holiday music push away at the memory of that night. When Candice did not move, nor remove her finders from his chest, he let his own touch wander to her stomach. "Or we could talk about this," he said, not touching the location of the scar, but still indicating it.

Candice paled and stepped back a tiny distance. Her eyes shadowed with old pain and her face lost some of its bright color. "What-?" she began to ask.

"I noticed it," Adam said as gently as his hard, rough voice allowed. "Back at the Waystation, when you'd reach up for something in front of me or just happen to adjust that t-shirt the owner makes you wear. When you'd show off just a little bit of that stomach of yours." Although he did not mean for it, his normally-harsh voice had become softer, and heavy with a hint of desire and appreciation.

Candice actually blushed, a shift from her normally-worldly attitude that brough a rise of something warm in Adam. "I don't know what you mean," she nearly sputtered. The bartender walked forward, leading him on and around the edge of the open area at the front of the market. Space had been cleared around the large tree raised in front of City Hall. "A good girl doesn't lead on a man like that."

"Uh-huh." Adam resumed his place beside her, following as they meandered. "Well, while you weren't showing me things I wanted to see, I saw part of the scar."

"It's…" words failed her.

"A long story?" Adam guessed, knowing the feeling. "A hard one to tell?"

"We've all got baggage," Candice whispered. She stopped and turned to face him. "Tell you what, cowboy, show me yours and I'll show you mine." This, the bartender said with the faintest upturn of her full lips.

They were standing near a group of carolers dressed in mock Victorian garb. Adam looked at them and closed his eyes, forcing his voice back to the comfortable security of emotionless facts. "London," he said, leading them away from the carolers' audience. "It was the 1960s, I think. Most of us don't really keep track of Human time in the Silver City." They moved away as the carolers took up a cheerful rendition of some imaginary reindeer. Adam and Candice continued on, back towards the vendors, and spotted Holly and the Twins. They were at a booth selling toys. "There was a girl," Adam said, his eyes on Holly and his steps coming to an abrupt halt. "A harpist. She was with the London orchestra. They were performing 'War Requiem' at Saint Paul's Cathedral."

Holly saw them slowly approaching and waved. Candice waved back, but remained beside Adam. "You told me you were an Angel of Destruction," the bartender recalled. "Were you supposed to…"

"No. I wasn't there for her." Adam took a deep breath of the cold night air, wishing Winter would just get on with it. "I was there for her parents. They were… like the *Drest-Vidar*. Like Holly's parents. They were getting ready for a ceremony, a ritual sacrifice. They wanted power and were willing to…" His eyes remained on Holly.

Candice followed the look and had to visibly suppressed a gasp. "Like Holly's parents?"

"Nothing changes," Adam growled. "It's the same damn story, again and again."

"So you were supposed to stop them?"

The warrior shook his head. "No. Free Will. I couldn't stop them. The Chorus sent me to watch and wait. If the parents did it, if they killed their own daughter, then I'd be free to… do my thing."

"Is that how it worked?" Candice asked. "You get sent somewhere to watch people, and if they do somethin' bad, you punished them?"

"No. It was never like that." Adam looked up with closed eyes, forcing down all the blood-soaked centuries. "I never really interacted with Humans. I stayed in the Silver City until I was called on. By the time I showed up, the deed was done and Judgement was made. I just went in, did my thing, and left. I never waited around."

"You never got to know us," Candice realized. "Never saw us except when you were… doin' your thing."

"I never wanted to," the warrior countered. "I saw plenty while I was down here. I didn't want to see more."

"So, what was different about that time?"

Adam shrugged. "No idea. For some reason, the Chorus sent me to London and told me to wait." He shook his head angrily. "It should've been Simkiel or one of his kind. They're the Watchers, not me." Water was forming in his eyes, and this only made him angrier. "They're the ones who spend all their time here, supposedly keeping an eye on things."

"Was that the first time you'd spent a while among us?"

The warrior nodded, sniffing back the emotion that threatened to break out of his control. "The girl's orchestra was performing 'War Requiem' that night," he recalled. "I was in the cathedral, just waiting for some idiot reason, so I got to hear the whole thing. After..."

"The girl died." It was not a question, but Adam shook his head slightly.

"I broke my orders," the warrior admitted in a hollow voice. "I tried to save the girl. I took her to Epping Forest, to Elizabeth's Hunting Cottage." He laughed without humor, then, looking down at his scarred hands. The left still carried the burn scars from his rescue of Holly from her parents, and the right bore the puncture scar from his confrontation with the *Drest-Vidar*. "I had to take a physical body," he recalled, flexing his hands and noting again the loss of dexterity in both. "Like this one, actually."

He looked up with hollow eyes, seeing only the past. "Her parents had a grimoire." Adam glanced at Candice. "You know what those are?"

The bartender nodded. "Holly told me."

"Her parents used it. It had my True Name. They still needed her blood to finish the ritual." His empty eyes were still locked with Candice's. "They made me do it," was all he said.

The bartender stood in front of Adam and took his large, damaged hands in her own. The warrior noticed, then, that her hands, though not scarred, were calloused. A lifetime of work and living had left their mark on Candice. Somehow, though, this had not hardened those hands. Her palms and her fingers remained soft, gentle, and accepting. She held his hands in hers and said nothing.

"They thought I was under their control," Adam almost whispered, "They didn't realize that they had to keep giving orders or imprison me. So I... did my thing. After that, though, I couldn't do it anymore. Eventually, the Chorus gave me another assignment, but I... I just couldn't."

"So you were sent here."

"A little more complicated but, yeah. Basically."

They stood for some unknown while like that. Neither said anything, and neither tried to force the issue. Candice kept his hands in hers, and he kept her eyes in his. Somehow, for some unknowable reason, Winter kept Her storm at bay, allowing the moment to go on for as long as it needed. The bartender pulled his hands to her heart, her eyes and his flowing together. They were nearly the same height, though Candice did need to look up just slightly. Their heads moved closer, until their breath became as intertwined as their fingers and their eyes. Her lips were very smooth, a small part of Adam's mind noticed as they made one more point of contact. This felt, to his warrior's mind, as though velvet was wrapping itself around raw iron. She opened to him, her breath like a summer wind on the dying embers in his chest. The very tips of their tongues caressed, tentatively. They both tasted the cider from before, as Adam hesitantly reached out. Candice sensed his hesitance, his inexperience, and led them both in this deeper exploration.

After a time, they parted, though hands remained clasped over her heart. "Well," she said breathlessly. "You showed me yours..." Candice had not been completely swept away by what they had just done. Her voice carried great reluctance, but a willingness to open her pain to Adam. Her eyes feel away from his as she spoke, the shame of her past weighing them down.

The warrior reached up with both their hands, raising her gaze back to his. "You only ever have to show me what you want me to see," he promised.

They continued swimming in each other's eyes, but eventually, Holly and the Twins approached. They were loaded down with foolish toys and sweets and filled to overflowing with holiday cheer. Marun stopped short as the small group approached, staring at Adam and seeing beyond the surface. She whispered to her sister and they both held Holly back.

"Why don't we get a good spot for the lighting?" Harun suggested, turning Holly away, overriding her objections.

"We'll hold a spot for you," Marun offered.

"No," Adam replied. He turned slightly, though he made no move to disengage with Candice. "Together," was all he said.

6

Most of the celebrants had already gathered around the large tree in the center of City Hall's great lawn. Infants were being hoisted onto father's shoulders while mothers worked valiantly, but flutily, to maintain some control over the older, more ambulatory children. The commercial holiday music had stopped, replaced by the excited din of the people. Several city officials had gathered atop the stage, suited bureaucrats with uniformed representatives from the Fire and Police Departments. Even the hired Santa Claus had joined with this collection of esteemed local dignitaries.

Alongside Disanté's leaders, Adam spotted Lilith Aubrey standing on the stage. The warrior was not surprised to see the local ruler of the Agarés Corporation and true overlord of Meropis County, but he was surprised at her appearance. She was dressed, as always, in an impeccably-fashionable, but practical, suit. Her pants and coat shielded her narrow frame from the deepening cold. Her mass of light brown hair was bound in a rigid bun at the back of her head. Her dark-framed glasses rested against her face as her gaze darted around the area. This, Adam realized, was the surprise. Aubrey was scared.

Nearly from the moment of his arrival in Meropis County, Adam had heard of the terror that was Aubrey's wrath. Time and again, men were ruined, small businesses destroyed, and obstacles ruthlessly removed. As the regional vice president of Agarés, Lilith Aubrey was the most powerful person in Central Texas, owning both local politicians and law enforcers. She had a reputation for being all-powerful, all-seeing, and without mercy.

The woman standing atop the stage now was someone else entirely.

"What is it?" Candice asked, leaning closer so that her words needed only to float the tiny distance to embrace Adam's ear.

The warrior narrowed his eyes, seeing past the flesh. "Something," he muttered. Aubrey stood rigid, frozen and suspended. Her hands shook slightly, almost unnoticeably. Already fair-skinned, her face was even paler than normal. Normally, Agarés' local leader was surrounded with security. These were present, Adam noted, but different. They did not move like protectors, with senses reaching out for potential dangers. Instead, these strongmen were oriented towards Aubrey herself, like jailors keeping watch over a prisoner.

With Aubrey stood two men. These, Adam did not know. They were tall and well-built, fair of face and hair. Their clothes were cut to enhance their arms and chests. Several women, and more than a few men, in the area kept glancing at the two men as though drawn to them. Even Holly and the Twins, normally almost oblivious to men, kept sneaking glances at the two, an air of quiet lust drifting amidst the festive crowd. They were very similar, Adam noted, both in appearance and demeanor. Not quite as identical as the Twins, there was nonetheless an obvious familial tie to these two men. Adam blinked, and finally saw the same similarity to Aubrey.

Her eyes, having been darting through the crowd, at last found Adam's. Tears emerged for only a moment, and a brief flush of color appeared in her face. The warrior had spent countless centuries seeing the doomed eyes of his victims. He knew the look of someone confronted with their ill-fate. He saw that now in Aubrey. She looked to him for some escape from whatever her beautiful siblings had brought, but then that shadow of hope vanished when one last group stepped onto the stage.

"Look who's here," Holly muttered.

Adam looked and spotted Justin Cade, the something-or-other to the City Manager. The potato of a man waddled, as always, with puffed-up self-importance. He did little to hide his sneer at the assembled crowd, and even looked as though he had smelled something uncouth. Adm recalled seeing the same look, the same dismissive superiority, in princes throughout time. He stepped aside as another man took the stage, this one tall and utterly forgettable. "Who's that?" Adam asked.

"That's the mayor," Marun replied.

"For one more year, at least," Harun noted. The Twins glanced at each other, having another of their silent conversations. Harun kept glancing towards Adam as though she wanted to say something, but Marun pressed her lips together, demanding silence.

"Just spit it out," Adam grumbled, trying to parse the source of Aubrey's fear. She was glancing towards the Mayor's small group, but her eyes were not on any of the men currently standing atop the stage. She looked back to Adam and made as though to lean forward. One of her beautiful siblings put a hand on her arm, pulling her back the fraction of a breath she had leaned forward. The other whispered something in her ear, and the feared vice president of Agarés lowered her gaze.

"We need to tell him," Harun insisted.

"You know what he'll do!" Marun almost hissed.

"But he's here tonight!"

"He won't get on the stage!"

"He's right over there!"

"Will you two just stop!" Adam barked. "Spit it out or shut up."

The Twins shared one more concerned look. They were about to speak, but Holly interrupted them. "Who's that?" she asked, nodding back towards the stage.

Adam looked, and froze.

A man walked up to stand beside the Mayor. His body was unremarkable, as unremarkable as Adam's. He had always managed to blend into the background, the warrior knew. He disappeared into the crowd, all the better to do his job. The man leaned slightly and whispered into the Mayor's ear. The elected official made no move to acknowledge, instead letting the words slither into his soul. This was a fact of the Fallen, Adam understood. Their natures did not change, even after being imprisoned in Human flesh. The Twins had always been creatures of information, of gossip and debate. This remained true, even when they were condemned to the bodies of these women. So it was with Za'afiel; he was a warrior, a being of violence. This had not changed with the birth of Adam Kadmon. This had not changed with whatever the man on the stage called himself.

"Orobas," Adam seethed.

The Twins moved to stand in front of Adam, trying to block his line of sight. "He's been here a long time," Harun said gently.

"A lot longer than you or us," Marun said firmly.

"He's been a part of this town for as long as it's been here. Longer."

"He helped build it."

"We assumed you knew."

Adam snapped his eyes to each of the Twins.

"No, we didn't," they conceded.

"Who is he?" Candice asked.

"*What* is he?" Holly amended.

"He's a Fallen," Adam said grimly. On the stage, Orobas looked at Adam. he did not search, he was not scanning the crowd. The meeting of their eyes was not a happenstance. Orobas looked to exactly where Adam stood with the women he had sworn to protect, and he smiled.

"He's like you?" Candice asked.

"No," Holly said almost absently. "He's different."

"He's a Throne," Harun replied. "One of the highest orders."

"He was," Marun amended. "He Fell, just after the Rebellion. These days, he calls himself Jack Anwir. He's the City Manager, the one who actually runs the local government."

"Figures," Adam growled.

Orobas left the stage and walked around the lawn and the assembled crowd. As he moved, the people absently got out of his way, making a path without needing to be excused or ordered. The Fallen kept his eyes locked with Adam's as he moved, his gait easy and light. As he approached, Adam moved Holly, Candice, and the Twins back, away from the approaching Fallen and to dubious safety behind him.

The two Fallen stood before each other, more than an arm's length separating them. The air warmed from the hatred seething from these former Celestials. The twinkling lights overhead and all around dimmed and many shorted. On the stage, the Mayor began making a speech, the words lost upon the two men who started centuries of hatred at one another.

"Hello, old friend."

"It's been a while, Orobas."

"Thousands of years," the insidious Fallen agreed. "Right at the end of the Rebellion." The last hint of his good humor vanished. "You remember that, right? When you tried to purge me, to send me hurtling into the Pit?"

"Yeah," Adam said with utter darkness coming from the depths of his unwanted soul. "I missed."

Orobas leaned his head to the side, pulling at the collar of his winter coat and exposing a light scar that traced down the side of his neck. "Not by much."

Adam glanced to the stage, where the Disanté Mayor was still droning on about a season of forgiveness and brotherhood. "Still whispering to the powerful, I see," he noted.

Orobas shrugged. "We were all created to be what we are," he said with venom. "That's what you loyalists never understood. We could never be anything but what we were made to be." He jerked a thumb to his chest. "The Chorus made me an advisor. I was MADE to be the voice that counseled the powerful!"

"And you 'counseled' them," Harun said over Adam's shoulder.

"You 'advised' all those chieftains to become warlords!" Marun snapped over the other shoulder.

"And you're so different,' Orobas sneered at the Twins. "You whisper in their ears the same as me!"

"We encourage questioning!" Harun insisted. "We help them explore their world!"

"You corrupt them!" Marun agreed. "You turn them against each other!"

"Their pests!" Orobas said through gritted teeth. "Vermin! They deserve to be exterminated!" The dark Fallen cast a baleful look around the crowd, almost sneering his contempt for the people and their holiday joy. "What makes them so damned special?" he demanded. "Why do they get Free Will? Why do they deserve it? We served the Chorus! We maintain the order of Creation!" Orobas shook his head. "And what's our reward? Slavery! Entire Choirs get dedicated to serving these pests! We build them a paradise and all they do is ruin it, flinging their shit across this world!"

The dark Fallen jabbed a thumb as his chest. "All we did was ask a question!" this, he snorted in derision at the Twins. "For all your talk about encouraging questions, the moment some of your own siblings did it, you were the first to denounce us!"

"You didn't question," Marun objected. "You 'whispered' to Lucifer!"

"You incited a rebellion," Harun agreed.

"You weren't trying to redress some injustice."

"You wanted to subvert the Chorus."

"To make yourself the overlord."

"I earned it!" Orobas nearly raged.

Adam narrowed his eyes at the barely-restrained outburst. Small details were beginning to assemble in his mind. Orobas was not just angry, he was almost shaking in rage mixed with something else. His eyes kept twitching, making an obvious effort not to look in a particular direction. The warrior saw this former councilor, this self-proclaimed master of Human desire and ambition, and decided to test a theory.

"What are you doing here, Orobas?" Adam asked. "What do you want?"

"What do *I* want?" He stood straight. "This is *my* town, Za'afiel! You came here, to the settlement I've spent centuries building. *You're* the intruder, the trespasser!"

"So, this is your town, huh?"

"I built it. It's mine. Just as I helped build the Garden and it *should've* been mine. Just as I directed the building of Enoch, of Nineveh and Jericho and Babylon. Just as I directed the raising of Egypt and Persia and Rome and all the others! They were all mine, and they were all taken away!" He glanced around the assembled Humans and outward, to the buildings of Disanté. "This is mine!"

"And who's taking it away?" Holly asked softly, stepping up beside Adam.

Orobas sneered at the girl, his eyes blazing hatred. Holly did not back away from the heat of that stare and its promise of obliteration. She stood her ground with a strange look of sadness, almost pity. "You built all those great places, and they were all taken away," she noted. "Is that your curse? The Fallen all seem to have some cost to their power." She glanced up at the Twins. "Trying to inspire curiosity, but building conspiracy theories. "She looked up at Adam. "Trying to isolate, only to be surrounded by people who need you."

The warrior looked away, grumbling an objection that died on his lips.

Holly looked back at Orobas. "You spent all of human history buildings these great cities, only to have them taken away. Now, you've spent generations building Disanté. Who's taking it away this time?"

Orobas' eyes became like miniature novae, and he gathered himself as though to lash out at this upstart Human. Adam took a half-step forward, putting himself firmly between the raging Fallen and the tiny girl. His gaze locked with Orobas' for several heartbeats. "You don't have your blades anymore," the dark Fallen pointed out. He gestured to the nearby police and private security. "I still have my full power. You can't beat me, can't stop me."

"Try," was all Adam said.

Another few heartbeats passed. Then, Orobas smiled. "I was never a warrior," he admitted. "You were the killer, the bringer of Destruction. You, and all your kind. I was only ever a simple advisor a… what was it you called me that last time? A petty bureaucrat." His voice had become mockingly small. "Of course, any good bureaucrat knows how to manage resources. Any good bureaucrat knows when to call in an expert."

Orobas leaned in conspiratorially. "You've been here for months, Za'afiel. Did you really think I wouldn't have a contingency ready? Did you really think I wouldn't be ready to settle our business? Do you think it's an accident that I reveal myself now?"

Adam's eyes narrowed as he, only now, understood the implied threat. The warrior took a step back, motioning for the women to do the same.

"Too late, old friend," Orobas mocked.

Golden light flooded the yard. The Mayor had finished his meaningless speech and signaled for the Christmas Tree to be lit. A thousand, thousand tiny, multi-colored lights blended together into a golden beacon. Perhaps it was a simple miscalculation by the engineers or the power supplies. Perhaps Adam's senses were particularly sensitive, given the threat of Orobas. Perhaps, the proximity of several Fallen and their centuries-long hatred for each other caused some mystical feedback. In any event, the Christmas Tree blazed as though it was on fire, its light amplified a hundred times over and forcing many of the celebrants to look away with startled exclamations. Only Adam and Orobas maintained their gaze, eyes locked on each other.

Orobas' smiled grew broader, more insidious and victorious. "I knew you couldn't stay quiet, Za'afiel," he gloated. "I knew, sooner or later, some Human would get hurt and you would come running. You and your idiot need to 'do the right thing.' You're pathetic.

"I knew you'd start causing problems, start attracting attention. I knew you'd draw someone in. All it took was my dropping a few hints, some minor revelation in the right ears. And he would come for you."

Orobas gestured towards the blazing tree, towards the miniature golden sun that had come into being. Adam looked and, for the first time in uncounted eons, he felt fear.

"You remember your brother, don't you?" Orobas gloated. "The only other Angel of Destruction to ever Fall?" The dark Fallen glanced at the figure. Standing before the blazing tree, he was a point of darkness in a sun, a blemish of hatred amidst the city's holiday cheer. "Chezef, you remember Za'afiel? The brother who betrayed you?"

Adam stepped forward, though only enough to put himself between the Fallen Angel of Destruction and the women. "Brother," Adam tried to say, helplessly against the memory of their conflict and the centuries of hatred that had resulted.

Chezef said nothing. He stood tall, equal to Adam. He wore a leather duster similar to his hated brother's, though his was dark, stained with countless miles of lonely wandering. The Fallen Angel of Destruction stared at Adam, mirrors reflecting one another, disappearing into each other amidst their shared history of violence. Chezef said nothing, he only pulled the edges of his long coat back, exposing the terrifying blades holstered on each of his legs.

Adam said nothing, he could say nothing, for there was nothing to say.

Orobas smiled again and backed away. "Well," he said happily. "I'll leave y'all to it."

7

"GET THEM OUT OF HERE!!!" Adam roared as he charged Chezef. His brother already had his hands on his blades, and was pulling them free. The crowd between them had parted a little; most Humans instinctively retreated from all the Angels of Destruction, even when those two were Fallen. This parting of the bystanders was suddenly exacerbated, though, when a mother spotted Chezef reaching for the terrible blades strapped to his legs and screamed, picking up her infant daughter and running. This scream was picked up by the remainder of the crowd, who also grabbed children and loved ones, trying to escape the cold fury of two Angels of Destruction.

Adam sensed the Twins behind, grabbing Holly and Candice and trying to pull them away. Both women objected, calling out to Adam, insisting on their intent to stay, to help, but his sisters understood that there could be no helping in this confrontation. Chezef was, like Adam, a Fallen Angel of Destruction. The Twins had seen, time and again over the countless centuries of Human civilization, one of these terrible beings unleashed upon the world. They had seen villages destroyed, cities ruined, armies slaughtered, and civilizations unmade. In each instance, there had only ever been a single Angel of Destruction present. Their Choir had been created as a final measure, an ultimate sanction against Creation, meant only for sparing use in the most extreme of situations. In all Celestial history, the Twins had only once ever seen more than a single Angel of Destruction unleashed, and that had been during the Rebellion.

But now, there were two in the same place, and at the same time. And those two were intent on destroying each other.

Winter fled from Adam as he charged his brother. There was no longer any cold, any building pressure of the coming storm. His breath no longer steamed in the air; his typical inner fire had been replaced with the cold of the Void. The ends of his long, white leather coat flapped in a new wind, one Adam himself generated as he darted forward, almost faster than a Human could see. The warrior no longer had his own blades; he had cast them aside months ago in order to rescue Holly from the *Ímā* Cult. If Chezef was able to draw his, the fight was almost certainly over. Their combat skills were equal, their experience also. Once, their murderous intent had also been equal, though that had changed.

Chezef looked at Adam as Za'afiel had once looked at his own victims. There was nothing behind those eyes. The unwanted soul forced upon all Fallen had withered in his brother. Where Holly and Candice and the Twins had fostered the soul of Adam Kadmon, Chezef had nothing like that in his undying mortal life. Adam had only been upon the Earth for a few months, not even a year, and already had burdened himself with sympathetic souls. Chezef had wandered this world for millennia, alone and hating. The cold fury, the barely-restrained violence that was at the heart of all Angels of Destruction still roared without a voice within Chezef. But in Adam, that need to destroy had become muted, tempered by the voices of the women in his mortal life, constantly whispering temperance.

The slightest shred of advantage only remained to Adam if he could close the distance, if he could end the battle before Chezef could draw his blades. So, in a blur that folded into the golden glow of Disanté's blazing Christmas Tree, Adam slipped away from the unwanted counsels of the women, whose unending sermons demanded mercy and forgiveness. Instead, the warrior called upon the fading embers of his black fire, his frozen inferno, and the violence returned as it always did, eager to be unleashed.

Chezef had only the barest fraction of a second to register his surprise. Victims did not charge at an Angel of Destruction, not even a Fallen one. They ran, they hid, they begged for an impossible mercy. But they never charged. Adam closed the distance separating them and lunged. Their heavy bodies impacted with such force that the blazing tree behind them shook in terror. Adam wrapped his arms around his brother and locked his fists together, pinning Chezef's arms at his sides, unable to continue drawing his blades. Adam meant to leverage this opening advantage, to pull his brother of his feet, but this could not be.

Chezef had his feet firmly planted and spaced. He, like Adam, was an immovable object. Even as his brother twisted and pulled, the Fallen Angel of Destruction only grunted a minor effort and released the grips of his blades. Inch by inch, Chezef worked one of his arms up and through the ring of Adam's interlocked limbs. The brother in black freed one arm and grabbed at the one in white. To an outside observer, the two would have seemed to be embracing, pulling each other closer in a rough hug. In truth, Chezef was leveraging against Adam, twisting his head down and pushing against his brother's, burrowing his scalp into Adam's face and breaking his concentration.

Their feet engaged in a twisted mockery of dance. The brothers reached out with their feet, their shins, and their knees. They lashed and jabbed, they maneuvered. Each sought leverage and position, even as their arms continued the false embrace. Finally, Chezef achieved what they had both sought. He suddenly hopped, nearly skipped, and wrapped one of his legs around Adam's, pushing forward with his equal weight and sending Adam to the unforgiving ground.

The fraction of a second Adam needed to regain his feet was all Chezef needed. The dark Fallen danced back, once more pulled back the edges of his black coat, and pulled free his blades. "NO!" Adam screamed, though not at his brother and the unleashing of those vessels of unfeeling destruction. His eyes were, instead, flashing behind and beyond his murderous brother.

Holly had not been pulled away. She had not taken the desperate seconds Adam had bought her with his life. Even as Harun had pulled Candice away, towards their truck, Holly was running away from Marun, having easily slipped out of the larger woman's grip. Adam's stubborn partner was, even as she ran forward, pulling her small pistol from the equally-tiny holster beneath her overlarge sweater, at the small of her back. She dropped to a knee and sighted, firing at Chezef.

Adam's Fallen brother turned with inhuman speed and spun his blades. Like Adam's lost weapons, Chezef's were one-sided, with the sharpened edge held away from the arm. The hilts stuck out, perpendicular to the blades, so that even as the wielder kept his hands at his sides, the blades continued along the line of his arms. The terrifying weapons had the name of their owner, the only being in all Creation who could employ them, engraved along their metal in the glyphs of the First Language. With a flick of the wrist, Chezef rolled the blades around, so they rested against his arms, as he turned to face Adam's partner.

Holly's bullets lanced out with perfect accuracy. She had incredible skill with her chosen firearm, naturally dexterous. After all the hours she had spent in the past months at a firing range, that skill had only grown. Her shots should have taken Chezef in the flesh of the arm and the leg. In any mortal opponent, they would have.

Chezef spun his blades in practiced, graceful movements. Whereas Adam was the charging beast, the lunging predator in their Chorus, his brother had always been the dancer. As Za'afiel, he had been the stronger of the two, but Chezef had always been the faster. His blades whirled around, catching Holly's bullets, brushing them aside long before they could find their owner's vulnerable Human body.

The dark Fallen took a single step forward, towards Holly. This motion, this barest of threats to her, was enough. Adam roared and leapt onto his brother. He wrapped his arms around Chezef's torso and heaved, sending the dark Fallen tumbling back and away from Holly.

"I told you to run, dammit!" Adam barked as he ducked the blind slash of one of Chezef's blades, made as the dark Fallen tumbled away from Holly.

Marun tried to grab Holly from behind, but the much-smaller girl ducked and tumbled to the side in a move Adam had drilled into her only a few weeks ago. She combined this with her own repetitive practice of reloading her gun, ejecting a spent magazine from the weapon's well and pulling the spare out. In one perfect motion, Holly had tumbled away from Marun, came back to her knee, and reloaded her weapon, already taking aim at Chezef. "I'm not leaving!" she declared in a voice that could have stopped a changing tide.

Chezef had already regained his feet and was reorienting on his brother, swiping away more of Holly's shots without so much as a sideward glance at the Human. "Get Candice somewhere safe!" he barked at Marun, who nodded and left.

"Adam!" Candice called, even as Harun was pulling her into the waiting truck.

"Just go!" the warrior called out, not taking his eyes from the advancing Chezef.

The pair of Fallen Angels of Destruction, one armed and one not, circled each other. Adam did not bother pulling out his knife. It was a mortal weapon, and would do nothing against Chezef's blades. No weapon in all Creation could stand against an armed Angel of Destruction, so Adam kept his hands free. They continued their circle, Chezef trying to close within reach of his spinning blades, and Adam determined to remain outside that lethal zone. Holly joined in this bizarre dance, maneuvering outside the brother's arena, staying at the edge of the great lawn, almost back within the vendor's booths, firing single, impotent shots whenever she had a clear sight upon their attacker.

Adam knew the longer this confrontation went on, the worse Holly and his chances were of surviving it. He relinquished conscious thought to instinct, to an eternal lifetime of battle and bloodletting. The warrior supplanted Adam Kadmon, letting the cautious mortal slip back in favor of the determined killer. The circle became a looping spiral as he drew Chezef into the lanes separating the vendor booths. Instead of the wide-open lawn, in which his opponent had every advantage, the warrior moved their engagement into narrower zones and the closer quarters more advantageous to his shorter area of attack.

Holly followed, keeping her gun sighted at Chezef. The combatants continued circling each other, but now in much tighter loops, she no longer had any open shots. She would not be given any clear chances, Adam knew, but this was an irrelevant disadvantage anyway. The warrior understood that, so long as Chezef carried his blades, her bullets would not be able to touch him anyway.

Chezef darted in, bringing one of his blades up and across his chest, intending to slash at Adam's throat. Rather than awaiting the attack, the warrior also darted in, closing the distance between them to nothing and raising a free arm up. He caught Chezef, grabbing his attack arm and spinning. Adam rolled into his brother, turning and grabbing the attacking arm with his other hand, as well, pulling at Chezef and sending him crashing into a nearby vendor booth. The dark Fallen was defeated for only a moment, though, rolling out of the crumbling booth and stabbing up at Adam's middle. The warrior deflected this feint and spun under and away from the real strike from Chezef's other blade.

The battle continued. Chezef slashed and Adam dodged. The dark Fallen stabbed and the warrior deflected. When the blades came in for a double strike from above, they were met with a two-handed touch-block.

Chezef tried bringing his weapons to his chest and slashing them forward, but Adam bent backwards with more dexterity than even he knew his mortal body held, bending back and away from the strikes only to straighten and counter with quick double-jabs to his brother's chest and stomach. Chezef gasped and danced back. All Fallen were taken aback when their bodies felt pain; having spent so many eternities as Celestials, free of any such suffering, even centuries in a body still brought a moment of shock when nerve endings flashed their objection into fleshy brains.

The dark Fallen grimaced and lunged back in, stabbing forward with one of his blades. Adam skipped back, only to then twist and throw a cross jab with his off-hand, catching Chezef in the chin. His brother shook away a brief flash of stars and reversed his other blade, jabbing that fist up into Adam's middle. The warrior lost his air and stumbled back. Chezef slashed with one of his blades and caught his brother across the arm. The sleeve of the white leather coat took the attack, impervious even to a Celestial weapon. Chezef blinked when he did not see a fountain of blood come from his strike, but quickly recalculated.

Adam tried keeping his feet, tried backing away from his murderous brother, but he lost much of his dexterity along with his air, and was desperately trying to gasp it back into his chest. Chezef pressed this advantage, cutting one deadly probe after another as he forced Adam even more off his now-unsteady feet. The dark Fallen struck high, drawing his brother's defense up and exposing his middle again. Chezef used this and struck low with his other blade. Adam knew, just as his brother must have realized, that his blades could not penetrate the white leather coat. So, rather than trusting to the Celestial edge, Chezef was using his blades as blunt impact weapons. This latest attack carried none of the dark Fallen's normal grace and dexterity, instead transmitting only brute force. Adam's ribs cracked with the impact and what little breath he had regained rushed out of his body.

Chezef followed this with another high strike from one side, again drawing Adam's defense up. The warrior understood what was happening, but his head and neck were the only points vulnerable to the deadly blades, and he was forced to defend these, even as his brother landed one body-blow after another. Blood spurted from Adam's mouth. He felt more of his ribs give way. His legs grew unsteady, his vision blurred. Chezef kicked Adam's feet out from under him and the warrior fell to the ground.

The dark Fallen paused a moment, standing over his defeated brother. Adam looked up without blinking. This was centuries in the making, they both knew. Betrayals had stacked upon betrayals. This was the moment, more than any other, Adam suspected would come when he had Fallen to earth. He closed his eyes.

Shots rang out. Holly emptied the last of her rounds. This was useless, Adam knew, only delaying the inevitable. Chezef barely glanced at the girl, letting his blades defeat this pitiful, desperate, and final act. Adam glanced at Holly, hoping she would not carry his death, but fearing that she would. His tiny partner continued walking forward, spacing her few remaining shots out to make them last. She did not look defeated, though, but instead had the same, inflexible look Adam had come to learn meant she had not only decided on a plan of action, but was already enacting it. Holly put her fingers to her mouth and let fly with one of her ear-splitting whistles.

A roar shattered what remained of the Winter's power. All eyes turned to the far end of the vendors' booths as several of these were flung aside, shattering midair into a thousand, thousand fragments. Twin amber lights, formed into slitted eyes, shone upon the small group. Another mechanical roar, echoing a frustrated predator prevented from hunting within his own lands, gave challenge. The Beast charged at Chezef with murderous joy.

"What?" the dark Fallen had time to say before the Beast's impact.

The Beast spun at the last instant, swinging his rear wheel out and crashing against Chezef's body. The dark Fallen was sent hurtling away, spraying blood from his mouth as he was launched up and out, crashing into one vendor booth after another with enough fury to demolish half of the festival.

Holly ran up to Adam and supported him as he tried to regain his feet.

"I told you…" the warrior cut off his own useless words. Holly braced him against the Beast, where a fit of coughing spilled blood on the leather saddle. The motorcycle grumbled his indignant objections, but remained still as his rider gasped for air.

Sirens blared in the distance, drawing closer. Holly glanced in their direction, then back at the ruined vendor booths as movement disturbed the wreckage. She looked to her wounded partner. "What do we do?" she asked.

Adam also glanced at the sirens and then at where his murderous, unstoppable brother was already rousing himself. "He's after me," the warrior insisted. “I run, you hide.” He tried to grab the Beast’s throttle, but a stab of pain made him growl and nearly double-over.

“Yeah,” Holly sniffed. “Like hell.” She mounted the Beast and jabbed a thumb at the rear seat. “Get on.”

Adam made as though to protest, not only for her insistence on putting herself in danger, but for the indignity of what she was suggesting. “Would you shut the fuck up and get on!?!” she commanded.

The warrior had no choice. With another glance to where Chezef was struggling to free himself from the wreckage of his impact, Adam awkwardly swung a leg over the Beast and sat behind Holly.

“Let’s go, Beast!” Holly cried, hitting his clutch.

The Beast roared in agreement, rearing up before charging into the night.

8

"This is a bad idea," Adam grumbled, wincing as the medic applied bandages to his ribs.

"Oh, shut up and sit still," Holly replied dismissively. She put her phone back in a pocket of her white leather coat. "Frankie... Lieutenant Haymer, is in El Paso. She's coming back as fast as she can, but it'll still be hours."

They had fled the tree lighting, heading in no particular direction. Adam had tried grunting directions to Holly, insisting they get as far away as possible, but she had overridden him once again. A brief call with the Twins had brought their small group back together outside the offices of the *Daily Crier*, the building containing the sisters' local media empire. When the Beast roared into the parking lot and came to a halt, the jolt of the sudden stop had almost overwhelmed Adam, causing him to double over, spitting blood and nearly falling from the saddle. Candice had run to him from the building's front door, catching the heavy man before he could fall to the ground and helping him down. She had cradled Adam in her lap, demanding they call for help.

"Haven't seen you this bad since summer," Isandro noted. He had been Holly's first call, arriving nearly at the same time as the ambulance. The good cop had brought with him his entire squad and secured the area as best any Humans could, with lights flashing and weapons visible.

"It won't keep him away," Adam grunted, trying to order the collateral damage away.

"How is he, Jason?" Holly asked, ignoring her partner, as usual.

"He'll live," the medic apparently named Jason replied. He was the same one who had treated Adam after their confrontation with the *Drest-Vidar* weeks ago. For some reason, Holly had his contact information and had summoned him, along with Isandro. The young man had arrived in his ambulance, needing little prompting to begin his treatment of Adam. The medic named Jason had already given the warrior something for the pain, though it only dulled somewhat the difficult process of bandaging the cracked ribs. "He needs to limit his movement for the next few days, though."

"Can't," Adam grunted against the pressure the medic was applying. His treatment had begun with stripping to the waist. He had objected, tried to put his foot down, tried to assert his own Free Will, but once again, the women in his life had overridden him. Candace and Holly had all but shoved him into the back of Jason's ambulance, and together they stripped him of his coat and his red flannel shirt.

This had been almost unbearable to Adam. As Za'afiel, he had born his self-inflicted marks with… not pride, but rather public shame. The Twins knew of the marks, of course; they, like all the Angels, knew of his habit of carving his victims' names into himself. His rare appearances amongst the other Celestials always caused whispers, as eyes were drawn to the names he had inscribed into himself. As Adam, he had kept the marks covered. In fact, as he sat, exposed to all, he realized that only two sets of eyes had ever seen them.

Candace did not recoil as she should from the names. Her eyes did not even register their presence, instead remaining fixed on Adam's. She had seen them before, of course. During his battle against the *Ímā* Cult, she had tended his wounds; she had seen him stripped to the waist, just as he was stripped now. The bartender had bandaged him without comment, without demand for an explanation, even as her fingers had traced along the strange designs of the First Language. Afterward, Candace had never made comment about the names. She had never forced the issue.

Holly was another matter, of course. After she had seen the names, when Adam had thoughtlessly exposed his crimes to her, she had been forever probing. The warrior glanced at her as Jason the medic continued his healer's work. Once more, her eyes were drifting over the names, those twin pools of midnight flowing across the loops, spirals, and diagonals as they wound across his mortal flesh. Once more, when caught, she overcompensated, seeming to look away as though she were inspecting everything in her area. As they lived together, she often saw him in overly-loose shirts or after showering. Like Candace, she never gave voice to her questions, but they were always there, just behind her painted lips.

Now, sitting in the back of an ambulance, stewing at the time all this was taking, Adam was exposed. Isandro had only whistled when he saw the names. "That must've taken awhile," was all he had said, and only gotten a grunt from Adam in reply. Again and again, one of his cops would come to the back of the ambulance, giving their commanding officer some report. Each time, the person's eyes lingered on Adam's torso and arms, on the visible marks of his centuries of horror and death. Everyone saw, everyone stared. No one asked.

"So, he's your brother?" Holly asked.

Adam grunted.

"Chezef was an Angel of Destruction," Marun said sadly.

"Like our big brother," Harun added.

The Twins were also standing at the back of the ambulance, near to Isandro and often speaking quietly with him. They had been unusually quiet at the little gathering, only watching Adam be tended to. Their usual stream-of-consciousness commentary was silent, their matching eyes filled with worry, as blood had been wiped away, cuts and bruises mended, and pain eased.

"He was the first to Fall, after the Rebellion," Harun noted.

"He was the first to Fall voluntarily," Marun almost whispered.

"That can happen?" Holly started.

The Twins nodded. "It's rare," they replied.

"But it does happen."

"For most, transubstantiation is a punishment."

"If an Angel disobeys the Chorus, or fails in their duty, there's a trial."

"If a majority votes to convict, the Angel is either condemned to the Pit, or they're sent to Earth in a mortal body."

"Sometimes it's an escape hatch," Adam said, his voice a mixture of regretful growl and ashamed whisper.

Holly glanced her question to the Twins.

"If an accused Angel doesn't want to face their trial," Harun explained.

"Or is already condemned, and fleeing one of the Angels of Destruction," Marun added, with a sorrowful glance to Adam.

He did not mean to touch the name. In fact, all the time Adam was sitting, exposed, in the back of Jason's ambulance, the warrior had been making a conscious effort not to touch or look at the name. But, with the damning insistence of memory, his fingers went to his heart. Nearly all the names were packed closely on his mortal flesh. Although never touching, the damning list of Za'afiel's crimes, of his victims, were nonetheless bound closely together. From a distance, the entries in the First Language blended together, as all sins do, darkening Adam's torso and arms. Within this horrid declaration of failures, though, one name was separate.

Over his heart, one name held a particular place of shame. This entry did not spiral or loop. It did not coil within another name, nor wrap itself around one. This one did not join in a mockery of geometry. Within the rolling dialogue of the First Language, forever burned onto his body, there was a gap. One point of emptiness rested over Adam's heart, one spot untouched by the dark writing. Within this void was a single name, a name that his fingers, his eyes, his unwanted soul could not avoid.

"Is that?" Candace whispered.

"Chezef," Marun read.

"The first of the names," Harun agreed, tears as much in her voice as in her soft eyes.

"They sent me to bring him in for trial," Adam whispered, a glob of something rancid sticking in his throat, rising to his eyes. "I could've said no, but I didn't."

"Chezef transubstantiated, rather than face trial," Marun said.

"There was a lot of that, after the Rebellion," Harun noted.

"So, he escaped?" Holly asked.

The Twins nodded. "Free Will," they explained.

"The ultimate sanction against Angels."

"Humans have the right of self-determination. No Angel can directly interfere, or otherwise help or harm, a mortal being."

"Is that what happened to-" Holly bit the question back. For weeks, since meeting the Twins, she had burned with curiosity about them, about their lives as Angels. What shred of modest curtesy she had normally kept those questions at bay, though.

Harun smiled through her sadness. "Angels are allowed to whisper," she said. "We can encourage you, just as Dark Angels can whisper temptations."

"We did a little too much influencing," Marun shrugged. "The Chorus said we'd gotten to… hands-on."

"Once Chezef transubstantiated, he was protected by Free Will."

"He wasn't the first of the Fallen, but he was among the first few."

"The Chorus mandated that we couldn't interact with Fallen. That they had to live in exile."

"So, your brother's been alone for… how long?" Candace's gentle voice was weighted with the possibility of endless lifetimes spent in isolation. She had remained at Adam's side as best she could during Jason's ministrations, even helping the medic in cleaning the scraps and cuts. Though Adam stiffened in silent complaint each time Jason the medic was forced to lay hands on one of the names burned into his flesh and soul, Candace caused no such recoil. Her fingers were as gentle as her eyes and her voice. She never lingered in either touch or gaze on Adam's many crimes.

"We tried reaching out to him," Harun insisted.

"As soon as we joined the Fallen, the first thing we did was try and make contact," Marun added.

"He refused."

"He didn't even acknowledge us. Or any other Fallen, for that matter."

"He's spent all these millennia just wandering."

"Waiting." The Twins' eyes fixed with Adam's.

"Chezef is out there," the warrior said, his voice hard and his hands forcibly moving away from the damning names. "He's looking for me. He won't stop, now that I'm vulnerable."

"I've got twenty good cops surrounding us," Isandro pointed out from outside the ambulance.

"You've got twenty bodies," Adam countered. "Waiting for their coffins."

"He's that dangerous?" Holly asked. She spent Adam's treatment sitting on the opposite side of the ambulance, grabbing items as Jason directed and obviously struggling to keep the worry from her large dark eyes.

"He's me," the warrior said simply. He glanced between Holly and Candice. "He's me, but without all… this." Adam waved a hand that encompassed them, the Twins and Isandro, and even the whole of Disanté. "Anything I can do, he can do better."

"He can't be stupid enough to take on all my people, all at once," Isandro insisted.

Adam looked to the good cop. "Do you remember this past summer?" he asked. "When Holly was taken? Do you remember all the damage I did?"

Isandro grunted in remembrance. Adam's path of destruction had nearly started a panic in Disanté as he tore the town apart in his search for Holly. "He can do all that?"

"He's me. But worse."

"What do we do?" Holly asked.

"Same options as always," Adam sighed, grunting as the medic named Jason applied another layer of bandages over his ribs. Despite the pain, the warrior was glad for the bandages. Besides the relief they offered his damaged ribs, he welcomed any covering of the names. "Run, fight, hide, or deal."

"You already tried fighting," Candice pointed out softly, breathing her comfort into Adam's unwanted soul.

"I can't beat him," the warrior grunted again. "Not while he's got his blades and I don't."

"Where are yours?" Holly asked.

"Still in that cave, I guess," Adam tried to shrug, but could not move his shoulders enough, especially from under Candice's soft hands.

"Could we get them?"

The warrior shook his head. "I didn't just drop them to rescue you, I forsook them. They're not mine anymore. Even if I tried picking them up, they wouldn't respond to me."

"Well," Isandro said mockingly. "That made a whole lot of no sense."

"It's more woo-woo stuff," Adam grumbled.

"So, no fighting," Holly considered, taking the spent bandages from Jason and replacing them in their proper place. "What about deal? What does he want?"

"Me," her partner replied.

"But why's he after you so hard?" Isandro asked. "What happened between you two?"

"Our big brother and the other Angels of Destruction sided with the loyalists," Harun smiled at Adam, who only turned away his eyes at the memory. Neither Za'afiel nor his mortal self ever spoke or even thought of the Rebellion. Of all the times in his eternal life, all the darkness and horrid memories, there was only one that carried with it more shame. Adam glanced again down at his torso, at the name marked over his heart.

"Chezef refused to fight," Marun said.

"He was the first Celestial to ever disobey an order."

"Uriel ordered all the Angels of Destruction into battle, to defend the Silver City."

"Chezef refused. He wouldn't take arms against another Celestial."

"He disappeared during the fighting."

"Uriel was furious," Marun said grimly, shaking her head.

"He never did have a sense of moderation," Harun agreed, laying a comforting head on her sister's shoulder.

"Probably why the Chorus put him in charge of the Angels of Destruction. A few other Celestials refused to fight as well, but Uriel took Chezef's refusal personally. After the fighting was done, he commanded that Chezef be brough to trial."

"Uriel wanted to make an example of him."

"But he refused to submit for trial."

Marun grimaced again. "So Uriel condemned him without a trial. He ordered…" Both of the Twins glanced at Adam, their expressions identical in their sadness for their brother. The warrior said nothing, only looked away, fighting, and failing, to keep his hand away from the name enshrouding his heart.

"Our big brother was sent to punish Chezef," Harun whispered.

"But he transubstantiated," Marun quickly added. "He escaped. He's been down here ever since."

"Waiting."

"So," Holly said firmly, "No fighting and no deal. That leaves running or hiding."

"No hiding," the warrior said, equally firmly. "Your parents tried to hide," he reminded his tiny partner. "Hide themselves and hide you." His eyes became hard, impossible to avoid and impossible to deny. "They failed."

Holly flushed, no doubt at the memory of the cave where her parents had tried to sacrifice her to a Dark Angel. As her thoughts often did when they went back to that dark cave, they would also go to Adam, slaughtering the cult that had followed her parents, just as he slaughtered her treacherous mother and father. "So, no hiding," Holly agreed in a shaky voice. "That leaves-"

"Run," Adam said with finality. He glanced at Jason the medic. "You done?"

The medic named Jason nodded. "Your mobility won't be anything great for weeks."

"Good enough." The warrior pulled on his blood-stained shirt and made as though to stand. The red flannel hid somewhat the damage to Adam's body, blending dark stains into the already dark patterns. Of greater importance, however, was the deeper pain the shirt concealed.

Candice held him back with a gentle touch. "What do you think you're doing?" she demanded in a voice that, though soft, held more steel than even Holly's.

"I'm leaving," Adam replied, though his voice lost just a bit of its unyielding stone. "He's after me. He only wants me. He'll follow. You'll be safe." He glanced at Holly. "You'll all be safe."

"Unless he comes after one of us, thinking we know where you've gone," Isandro pointed out.

"Not how we think," Adam disagreed. "He'll know I won't tell you where I'm going. He won't waste time asking questions that won't have answers. At most, he'll watch you for a few days, maybe a few weeks, in case I come back. I won't."

"Forget it," Holly said imperiously, standing and facing Adam. "You're not running away to die alone in some gutter. We're handling this together. We just need to figure out how," this last, she said with distraction as her complex mind began working.

Adam began to object, to try an assert himself, but Holly dismissively waved him to silence and Candice pulled him back to his seat with another impossibly-powerful touch that was as light as a feather.

"Why now?" she asked, looking to the Twins.

"Chezef was bound to show up at some point," Marun replied.

"Yes," Holly agreed, "but why now?"

"Orobas implied he had summoned Chezef," Harun pointed out. "He may have been lying."

"He never lies," Marun insisted. "He conceals, but he never lies."

"Would this… Orobas be able to just summon Chezef?" Holly asked.

The Twins shook their heads. "Whether Celestial or Fallen, no one commands an Angel of Destruction. Chezef himself proved that."

"Nobody puts baby in the corner," Isandro agreed.

"So, what? How did he get Chezef here, and why now?"

"Maybe it took him this long to find the guy," Isandro suggested with a shrug.

"We all knew where to find him," Harun said gently.

"He wasn't hiding," Marun agreed. "None of them do. The Angels of Destruction aren't very good at keeping a low profile." This last she said with a mocking grin to Adam.

"Ok," Holly mused. "So, again, why now? Orobas knew where to find him, and could probably leak Adam's location at any time. Chezef probably would have heard about Adam eventually anyway, right?"

The Twins nodded. "Word is already spreading about our big brother being here."

"We're doing what we can, keeping him away from the world's attention."

"But there are leaks. Word is spreading."

"So, Orobas wanted to control when this confrontation happened." She looked to Adam. "He wanted it now."

"But why?" Candace asked.

Adam leaned forward as much as his damaged ribs would allow, locking eyes with his tiny, imperious partner. "He wants me distracted," the warrior said, finally following Holly's line of thought.

"He wants both of us distracted," she amended. "Remember what Juan said last night? Word has gotten out about the both of us, working together. Distract one, and you distract both."

"But why now?" Adam repeated Holly's initial question.

Both then started. "The kid!" they said in unison.

9

"Now can I hit him?" Adam almost begged.

"Just stand over there!" Holly commanded, pointing imperiously at one corner.

Isandro had taken them to the police station and arranged for an interrogation of Juan. The tiny, would-be crimelord had taken one look at Adam and Holly and demanded his lawyer, which Isandro had continued to chuckle about as he shackled Juan to the bare table and left.

"I ain't sayin' nothin' without a lawyer!" Juan said again, sitting up straighter, the further Adam moved away. Sweat was already running in near-rivers from his brow and through the X-shaped scars across his face.

"We're not trying to get information for your prosecution," Holly said in her most reasonable voice. "We're only trying to find the little boy."

"The one you had locked in a closet!" Adam barked, taking a threatening step forward. Juan squeaked in terror and sunk into his chair, pulling against the chain shackling him to the metal table.

"Ahh!" Holly held up a finger in warning, then pointed Adam back to his corner. The warrior sullenly returned and threw an annoyed glance into the two-way mirror, almost feeling Isandro's amusement.

"Now look," Holly said, again adopting the reasonable tone she used with children and degenerates like Juan. "We've done this over and over and over. You know how this is going to end. You'll keep resisting and I'll finally be forced to let Adam loose." She stood and crossed around the table, approaching Juan. As short as the young woman was, she towered over the diminutive criminal. For the first time Adam could remember, Holly was able to use an advantage of height. She put one small fist on the table and the other on her hip, leaning a bit to stare down hard at Juan.

"But we've got a sort of time issue right now." Her voice dropped a little lower. Adam realized with a mix of surprise and pride that she was imitating his own habit of using a lower register to communicate threat. "I just can't do our little dance this time. So, I'm only going to ask you once, and then, I'm going to leave this room." She said this very calmly, with a glance back over her shoulder towards Adam. "He'll stay, though."

Holly leaned against the table and took a deep breath. "Who is the boy, and why did you take him?"

Juan glanced up at Holly, then at Adam. "I don't know who the kid was," he said.

Holly said nothing for a moment. Then, she sighed and stood, moving towards the door.

"I swear!" Juan sobbed. "I didn't know who he was! The *Drest-Vidar* had him! They were holding him! They wanted him for something!"

Holly turned and stared unflinching stone at Juan. "But why did you take him?"

"Because the *Drest-Vidar* wanted him! If they wanted him, he had to be valuable! I just figured I could hold him until I figured it out, or I could find a buyer!"

Holly glanced at Adam. "He's lying," she said.

The warrior nodded.

She sighed again and shook her head. "Do it," she said, leaving the room.

Adam waited until she was out and the door shut with a deadly click. The warrior then looked at Juan and smiled.

"I'm tellin' you the truth!" the liar lied, trying to pull away but held in place by the manacles. Adam helped him with this by grabbing the chain and slowly pulling it free of the table. He then kicked Juan's chair out from under the criminal. Juan tried calling for help, insisting that he had rights as Adam put a booted foot on the little man's chest. He grabbed Juan's manacled hands and pulled them apart, snapping the chain holding them together. "Alright! *Dios mio*, alight! The courthouse guy, Bailey! He hired me, contracted to get the boy!"

"Why?" Adam asked in a voice that would have shattered ice.

"I didn't ask!" Juan lied again. "I didn't care!"

Adam picked up the small-time criminal and threw him bodily onto the table. The warrior then grabbed Juan's right forearm with one hand and braced that shoulder with the other. "Why?" Adam asked gain as he joint-locked the right arm and began applying pressure.

Juan squealed an unintelligible answer, so Adam eased off a little. "What was that?" the warrior asked.

"Cade!" Juan yelled. "Justin fucking Cade! He put out the contract!"

"So, I'll ask again," Adam said. He then began a steady pressure, forcing the joint-locked right arm further and further against the tendons in that shoulder. "Why?" he drew out the word as he increased pressure.

"Aubrey, alright! Stop, fuckin' stop! I'll talk!"

Adam let go of the arm and once again picked Juan up. He dragged the weakly-squirming criminal across the floor to the two-sided mirror. He picked the little guy up and slammed him into the mirror, more for the entertainment of Isandro and his men than anything else. "What does Aubrey have to do with this?" he demanded.

"Aubrey wanted the kid!" Juan yelled, his face pressed against the window. "She had Agarés security people lookin' for him for weeks, ever since summer! She found the kid and was holding him, but the *Drest-Vidar* grabbed him and was hidin' him! When you beat them, Aubrey's people tried to get the kid back! Cade contracted to get the kid first and hold him!"

"Hold him?" Adam started. "Why? For how long?"

"Just 'till after Christmas!"

"Christmas? That was the date?"

Juan tried to squirm, but Adam only pressed him further into the window. "No," the criminal grunted against the glass. "They kept sayin' 'Winter Solstice,' but that's Christmas, right?"

"And after the solstice?" Adam pressed. "What then?"

"We'd give the kid to Cade! He said somethin' about somebody else wanting the kid!"

Adam dropped the criminal. He did not spare Juan either a look or a thought, but left him whimpering on the floor, where he had curled into a ball. Instead, the warrior left the room, nodding to two of Isandro's men, who were waiting to take Juan back to his cell. Adam moved to the nearby door which would lead into the observation room and entered. Inside, one of Isandro's men was collecting money from the others while the good cop spoke quietly with Holly.

"So, Aubrey's involved in all this too?" Isandro mused.

"More than involved," Holly countered, her eyes nearly lost as her mind rapidly danced through information and theory. "She seems to be central to the boy."

"She's at least part of the point," Adam confirmed. "It sounds like Orobas is having his agents deliberately counter her."

"Could that be why Aubrey was so scared at the tree lighting?" Holly guessed.

"The solstice isn't far off," Adam confirmed. "That was the deadline."

"But for what?" Isandro asked.

"For whatever the boy is for. Aubrey had until the solstice to get hold of the kid. From how she looked tonight, I'm guessing whoever she's in debt to isn't waiting anymore."

"Do we care?" Holly asked bluntly. "The boy is our responsibility, not Aubrey."

"You're right," Adam agreed. "Whatever Aubrey's into, she likely brought it on herself. The boy might be an innocent."

"Should we try to question her?"

The warrior shook his head. "Even if she talked to us, it would just be a waste of time. Kiliahoté has the kid. If Aubrey knew where to find him, she'd have Agarés security assaulting the place."

"So," Holly used. "We need to find someone the Agarés Corporation, with all its resources, can't."

"What now?" Isandro asked. "Do we wait for Frankie to get back, or do we try to find the kid ourselves?"

"The Rangers won't be here for hours yet, at the earliest," Adam noted. "Whatever's happening, something tells me it's going to be finished tonight." He glanced at Holly.

"Orobas arranged your reunion with Chezef tonight," she agreed. "So it's up to us. We need to find the little boy."

"Bailey."

"He's our only lead, right now."

"The only one we can pursue, anyway."

Isandro looked as though he would ask a question, but a sudden outcry pulled all their attention. They all filed out, into the large space assigned to Isandro's squad. Uniformed cops were all running towards the stairs at the opposite end of the large room. Most of them were already holding weapons, others were drawing theirs. Isandro stopped one and began asking, "What-" but was stopped at the sound of heavy gunfire.

A great many shots echoed up from the floors below. Shouts and curses joined in the firing, soon followed by the screams of the maimed and dying.

"Shit," Adam grunted.

"What the hell is it?" Isandro demanded, drawing is weapon.

Adam grabbed the good cop. "Me and Holly are leaving," he barked. "Don't try to stop him! Don't try to fight him! For damn sure don't try to arrest him! Disarm and walk up to him, slowly! Tell him everything you know! Don't try to hide anything; don't try to lie! Tell him everything we've just learned! EVERYTHING! Tell him Holly and I left out the back!"

"Where are you really going?" Isandro demanded as more gunfire and more screams tore up the stairs.

"Out the back!" Adam said again. Holly had already grabbed her helmet and his and was moving to the rear staircase. "Remember, don't try anything stupid or he'll kill all of you!"

Isandro stared a moment as Adam and Holly reached the door to the rear stairwell. "Won't he kill us anyway?"

"No," Adam grunted, shoving the door open for Holly. "He won't waste time and he won't hold grudges. Not against you, anyway. Just be honest and let him go. He'll leave."

Isandro reached for the radio at his belt. "I'll send some people with you," he offered.

"No!" Adam barked, about to follow Holly out. "It's just more bodies! We'll handle this! Keep your people out of it!"

The Beast roared as they reached the Disanté courthouse. His yellow eyes blazed like two miniature suns, illuminating Bailey as the little man had been walking to his car. Seeing who it was, the court clerk immediately dropped his briefcase and held his hands in the air. "I'll tell you anything you want!" he declared.

"Aww," Adam said regretfully.

The Beast also sounded sullen in the lowering of his growl.

"Just stop," Holly muttered as she dismounted, "both of you." Handing her helmet to Adam, she approached Bailey. "We can do this the easy way or-"

"I already said I'll talk," Bailey replied calmly, his hands still held out in full sight. "I have no interest in being persuaded by Mister Kadmon. I presume this has something to do with the boy?"

"Where is he?" Adam growled with the Beast offering his own grumbling emphasis.

"I haven't the slightest idea. I was paid to contract that Juan character to hold the boy until midnight tonight. When news of your final raid last night spread, Mister Cade from the City Manager's Office called me and cancelled the contract. I was paid my commission and that was the end of my involvement."

Holly approached Bailey, but kept a safe distance and left Adam a clear line of sight. She also, the warrior noticed, had her hand on her small pistol. "Why is everyone so interested in this boy?" she asked.

"Again, I'm not entirely sure," Bailey admitted. "All I was told, Lilith Aubrey of Agarés needed him. I was contracted by Mister Justin Cade to prevent her from delivering that boy to some unknown third party. Juan needed only hold him until midnight tonight, at which time Cade or one of his operatives would take charge of the boy. My involvement ended there."

"Delivered to who?" Adam asked. "Who was Aubrey going to give the boy to?"

"Someone from out of town," Bailey replied. "That's all I know for certain, though I had the impression that this someone was also from out of state, from very far away."

Holly returned to the Beast. "Now what?" she asked. "Do we try to question Aubrey?"

"No point." Adam was scanning the area, watching for any possible approach. "She's under guard. Likely we won't get close without a fight, and we can't afford to be in one place for too long. We do have one more lead on the boy, though. One more interested party."

Holly paused a moment. Then, "Kiliahoté."

Adam nodded. "Get on."

"Can I put my arms down?" Bailey asked.

Adam stopped the Beast more than a block away from Kiliahoté's house, silencing the engine. "What is it?" Holly asked, leaning in to whisper the question. She must have picked up on Adam's sudden tension. Even the Beast was still, alerted to danger.

Adam nodded at a non-descript van parked at the end of the road upon which Kiliahoté's house rested. "And there," he directed Holly's gaze towards another vehicle, this one on the opposite end of the street. Both vehicles were in view of the house, and together they had observation of all the possible entrances.

"Cops?" Holly asked.

Adam nodded. "Loyal to Orobas, most likely."

"They're looking for the boy, too," Holly mused.

"And haven't found him," Adam agreed. "Kiliahoté won't come here."

"Then why did we?"

"We're looking for a trail," the warrior shrugged slightly, testing against the bandages enfolding much of his torso. He was already healing, his Fallen body already mending itself. He was far from optimal, but he was increasingly mobile, and hoped that would be enough. "We need a starting point to track."

"So, where?" A soft melody played from Holly's pocket. She reached in and withdrew her phone, looking at the screen. "It's the Twins," she told Adam. "The cops were just at their offices. They ransacked the place. The entire building, actually.

"Orobas," Adam grunted.

"They tried the same at the ranch, but the Twins' private security held them off," Holly continued. "They think there's someone watching the ranch."

"What about…?"

"They still have Candace," she assured her partner, laying a tiny hand on his heavy shoulder. "They're all staying at the ranch, now. They want to know if we're coming."

"More bodies," Adam grunted, shaking his head. "Our only chance to head this off is to find the kid and leverage Orobas to try and call off Chezef."

Holly tapped on her phone. "They agree," she reported. "They're asking what our next move is."

Again, Adam shook his head. "If Chezef goes to them, I don't want them to know anything. We can't risk them. Tell them not to contact again. We're going dark."

Holly tapped again on her phone before putting it away. "So, what now?"

Adam nudge the Beast forward. "Let's start kicking up some rocks."

"Sorry, Mayonnaise," Delicious said with a shake of his enormous head. "You're only talking to me." Holly had called their contact within Junior's organization and arranged a meeting.

"Where's Junior?" Adam asked. The warrior's eyes were in non-stop motion, remaining aware of everything. They had met with Delicious at what was left of the Balls 'N Styx, Junior's entertainment venue. Several construction vehicles were scattered around the large parking lot, but all were silent and empty. The building itself was mid-demolition, with only a few traces of its iron skeleton still sticking up from the blackened hole that had resulted from Adam and Holly's last visit.

Delicious, Junior's massive enforcer and former doorman, watched Adam for a moment as the warrior kept watching the area. "Yeah," the near-giant muttered, "I heard about that."

"You heard about what?" Holly asked. Adam had insisted that she remain with the Beast, both for the protection the motorcycle could offer, and the fast escape.

"I heard the two of you had some serious heat coming after you. I heard about the tree lighting this evening."

"So you know I don't have a lot of time to dick around," Adam nearly growled. "Where's Junior?"

"At Telford, visiting his old man."

"When did that trip come up?"

"Just this evening, actually."

"That's convenient," Holly said dryly.

"No," Delicious replied, "that's smart." He turned his bulbous head towards the charred remains of the Balls 'N Styx. "When y'all start having problems, shit starts to get collateral, real fast."

"Hey, we didn't start the fire," Holly objected.

"No, but shit tends to get burnt when you two around." Delicious held up his giant, fleshy arms. "Look, no disrespect, but can we just get to this? I don't plan on being collateral, myself."

"Why are you still here?" Adam asked. "Why not go with Junior?"

"Told to stay. Besides, my mom lives here. She's got medical needs. I can't leave her, and I can't afford to move her."

"Fine," Adam grunted. "For two months, Junior's been feeding us locations on drug houses and kidnap victims. Why? Out of the goodness of his heart?"

Delicious snorted, sending the folds of his various chins waggling. "Junior never did nothing if there wasn't no profit."

"Competition," Holly said, her eyes narrowing and her mind calculating. Adam glanced at her. "We were clearing out his competition."

Adam looked back to Delicious. "Yeah, he figured y'all would figure it out eventually." The enormous criminal glanced at Holly. "Well, he figured the smart white girl would, anyway, not your dumb ass."

"I'm starting to get annoyed, Slim," Adam warned.

"Way I heard it, you ain't got time to stand around being annoyed."

"Fine," the warrior grunted. "What about that last house? We asked Junior to find us where the boy was being held, and he sent us around, busting all his competition. But why send us to that house last night? That correct house?"

"Junior had a meeting, night before last," Delicious said. "Lot of money changed hands. Yesterday morning, Junior told me to give you the right house."

"Who was the meeting with?" Holly asked.

"Not sure," the massive criminal admitted. "Official types. Government, I think. One of them called himself Cade."

Adam turned back to Holly and the Beast. She stared at him and nodded. "He used us to flush the boy out," she said in a soft voice.

"Yeah."

"Hey, Mayonnaise."

Adam glanced back.

The enormous man hesitated. "Look, man," he finally said, his deep voice softening. "On the streets, you got to do a lot to take care of yourself and your family." He breathed and closed his eyes. "You got to survive, know what I'm sayin'?"

"Better than most, Slim," Adam replied.

"But there's some things," Delicious paused. "There's got to be limits, you know? Why are all you official people so hot for this kid, anyway?"

"They are," Adam countered. "We're trying to help the kid."

"But why?"

"He called me," Holly answered. "On Halloween, he called me and he asked for help."

"That's it? Some kid asks for help, so you're helpin'?"

"Pretty much."

"What about you?" he asked of Adam.

The warrior shrugged and jerked a thumb at Holly. "She says we're helping the kid, so we're helping the kid."

"Yeah. Look, man. Junior didn't give two shits about this kid y'all're lookin' for. He used y'all to clear out some garbage. But… is this kid alone?"

"No," Adam admitted. "There's someone else who grabbed him."

"Does this someone know how the streets work?"

"Better than you or me."

Delicious nodded. "Then, if this someone was runnin' from everybody, from business and government, then there's only one person left in this town who might help."

"Who?" Holly asked.

"There's a lady. They call her Abuela. She runs a shelter, over on Sixth. She takes in runaways, junkies, people trying to hide. She doesn't answer to nobody. Everybody, even Junior, gives her respect."

"Why?" Adam asked.

"Not sure," Delicious shrugged. "She just… something about her."

"Thanks Slim," Adam said, mounting the Beast and holding the bike steady while Holly did so as well. Before the warrior spurred their ride forward though, Adam paused. "Hey, Slim," he called out.

Delicious, who had turned to leave, turned back.

Adm reached into the side pocket of his white leather coat and tossed a huge bundle of high-denomination bills to Delicious. "It's Christmas," he pointed out. "Take your mother on a trip."

10

"So," Holly murmured, "trap, right?"

Adam grunted, his eyes moving up and down the street. He had paused their approach to the shelter when he spotted two unmarked black vehicles. Holly had tapped him on the shoulder and indicated another two vehicles down the street, large transports with tinted windows and darkened interiors that did little to hide the large men inside.

G Street was quiet. This should have come as no surprise, since Disanté typically made little celebration during the year-end holidays. Even the bustling center of what passed for culture in Meropis County made only the most minimal changes in recognition for the season. The many restaurants, from the upscale French and Italian ones to the more cost-friendly chains, often only put out a single wreath or a few cheap paper Santa faces. The streetlights and traffic intersections were usually unadorned, offering only their harsh lights in a mockery of holiday cheer. The Performing Arts Center often even went dark during the holidays, as most performers offered some presentation of seasonal joy, which had been unwelcome in Disanté since the town's founding. In fact, the only concession this town typically made towards even recognizing the approach of Christmas were the gaudy signs in front of the many shops declaring year-end bargains. That was how Disanté was supposed to mark the holiday.

But something had changed this year. As the year wound down, Adam and Holly had noticed a marked upswell in community festivity. The streetlights had all been adorned with glittering wreaths. Nearly every storefront was decorated with garland and lights. Restaurants, rich or common, had made efforts towards a variety of seasonal themes, from child-centered displays of Santa and snowmen to conservative reflections of Dickensian moods. The apartments above the many storefronts along G Street showed lights, wreaths, shining Christmas trees, and glowing menorahs. For weeks, holiday music had drifted upon the urban breeze, somehow blending together into a festive greeting. Adam had made little of this change to Disanté, though Holly, Candace, and the Twins had seemed greatly surprised. Without coordination, without planning or preparation, the people of Disanté began reveling in seasonal joy.

But this night was quiet and dark. The worsening cold pushed against the town. Breath frosted in the air. Winter's needles prickled on exposed flesh. Dark clouds encircled Disanté. The twinkling lights in the streetlight garlands and in apartment windows seemed muted, flickering as though on the verge of being snuffed out. There was no music, nor any other sound, but for the cold wind clawing at their heads. Although they were only a few hours since sundown, no holiday shoppers wandered the stores, and no celebrants visited the restaurants. The Performing Arts Center had, for weeks, advertised a children's choir singing holiday cheer that night, but the tall building of glass was dark and still. Something had placed a dull blanket over G Street, attempting to smother the kindling festivity.

"Look there," Adam said, nodding to a pair of cargo trucks parked across the street from the shelter.

Holly looked where he directed. "What is it?" she asked, noticing nothing.

"Delivery or moving trucks at night?" Adam pointed out. He then looked once more up and down the dark, quiet street. "And isn't this supposed to be the dinner rush?"

"What do we do?" she asked quietly.

"If they haven't spotted us yet, they will." He looked up and down the street. There were few alleys or unlit parking lots. G Street had been intended as a cultural hub, bright and welcoming. They had ridden the Beast up to the nearly-abandoned church and parked, as that was the only dark point on the annoyingly well-lit street. For at least three blocks in any direction of the shelter, unnoticed movement would be all but impossible. "Well," Adam sighed, dismounting, "when in doubt, be bold." He helped Holly dismount as well. "If nothing else, we'll confuse them for a few minutes by not sneaking."

"We'll need to be quick, either way," Holly pointed out as they walked up the sidewalk towards the shelter. Her eyes were darting up and down

G Street. There was no sign yet of Chezef. Adam knew, though, that there would not be until his brother arrived.

They walked up the sidewalk, Adam directing their course so that it went straight past one of the suspicious vehicles.

"Aren't cop cars supposed to be marked?" Holly asked.

"Not always," Adam grunted. Four men were inside that dark vehicle. The front passenger had surveillance equipment and all were armed. All four of the men had looked at Adam and Holly, clearly taken aback at how boldly the pair walked past them. The men had badges and bold signs displaying "POLICE" across their chests. All of them had covered their faces, but Adam suspected their intent was not to protect themselves from the worsening cold.

"Isandro says Special Tactics has been deployed," Holly reported, tapping on her phone. "But he doesn't know for what, or by whose order."

"Orobas again," Adam rumbled as they approached the front of the shelter. "He's shadowing us." The warrior paused outside a closed jewelry store.

"What?" Holly asked.

"We're doing exactly what Orobas wants," the warrior almost growled. "We're leading him to the kid."

"Do we walk away?" Holly asked. "If Kilihoté has kept the boy safe until now…"

Adam grimaced and looked up and down the street. There was still no sign of Chezef, but that would not… that could not last. "Not many options left," the warrior sighed. "If you won't let me leave town, then this is our only path. Plus, we've already led them here." He glanced at Holly, about to try once more to convince her that his leaving was for the best, but any argument died, crashing against her narrowed eyes and undeniable will.

The building was just as festively-decorated as the other shops and homes along G Street. There were no windows on the ground floor, but the two upper stories were bright from within, and even from the street they could see holiday décor. A large bulletin board was to the side of the front doors, with notices of missing children and contact information for free legal assistance. At one end of the building was a sign directing people towards the entrance of a free clinic, though this was unlit.

Holly stifled a gasp as the pair approached the quiet building. Adam spun, but saw no immediate threat. Instead, she was standing rigid, leaning back as though as though a sudden, strong wind had thrust upon her. Her large, dark eyes were unfocused and half closed, and her head weaved back and forth just slightly. Adam reached out and put a steadying hand on her arm. "Breathe," he commanded. "Tell me."

"You can't feel it?" she breathed, her eyes fluttering closed.

Adam turned back to the quiet building. Months ago, to rescue Holly from torturous death at the hands of a Dark Angel, Adam had severed the last of his connection to the otherworldly. He had said nothing to her, to anyone, about this handicap. He tried never even to talk about how debilitated he felt in the months since, no longer to sense anything beyond the limited five senses of his Human body. He concentrated, trying to push past how limited he had become, but felt nothing.

"There's something here," Holly breathed.

"Hostile?"

She glanced up at him. "How do I tell?"

"Clear your head," he instructed, keeping his hand on her arm. "Let go of questions. Just let whatever it is flow past." She did as he directed, breathing deeply and closing her eyes. "In one word," Adam said, "what do you feel?"

"Welcome," Holly whispered, then blinked her confusion at the word.

Adam glanced back at the building and grimaced. "Well," he almost growled, "that's something, anyway."

"Isn't that a good thing?" she asked, nodding him away and standing as tall as she could.

"A spider is welcoming of a fly," the warrior pointed out, turning back to the building.

Before they could take three steps towards the front door, it opened. A young woman, dark skinned and conservatively dressed, leaned out. "She's waiting for you," the young woman said, nodding for them to enter.

Adam and Holly grimaced at each other and walked in. The young woman closed and locked the door. The interior was spacious and open. Game tables were intermixed with large couches and a great many bookshelves. Some areas had been dedicated for classes, with large boards and chairs. Other places had been cleared of any furniture, instead bearing soft carpets and cushions piled one atop the other. At the distant corner of the building was a set of double doors with marking indicating that the free clinic lay beyond. Along the far right wall, there was a tall set of counters upon which rested clipboards, boxes, and various small electronics. Adam saw no immediate threat, but he did not relax as the young woman led them towards the opposite end of the room and a large staircase.

"You used to work at the Balls 'N Styx," Holly pointed out.

The young woman glanced at her and nodded. "I didn't think you'd remember me," she said.

"It was the night of the fire, right?" Holly replied. "You were one of the waitresses."

The young woman nodded. "I got pregnant my junior year, and my boyfriend dumped me." She stifled a slight sob. "He said it wasn't his, that I'd cheated on him. He told everybody. I dropped out, but getting a job wasn't easy, unless I wanted to flip burgers for pennies. My mom threw me out; I lost the baby. Junior was the only one who offered to take me in and give me a chance."

"You didn't know what he would want in exchange?" Adam said. He tried not to make his words accusational or condescending, but Holly still punched him in the arm.

"I knew," the young woman replied. They reached the base of the staircase and she turned to face Adam. "Everyone knows what Junior is. But at least with him, I wouldn't be walking the streets." She turned and began leading them up the stairs. "After you two burnt down the Balls 'N Styx-"

"We didn't start that fire," Holly insisted, not for the first time.

The young woman shrugged. "After the fire, Junior told all of us that we could either wait for him to reopen another place, or we could go to work at one of his houses."

"Houses?" Holly asked.

"Brothels," Adam almost growled.

"Whorehouses," the young woman corrected as they reached the first landing and kept ascending. The rear wall was a tall window looking out on the narrow balcony of the apartment building behind the shelter. Those windows were dark, save for a small Christmas tree twinkling against the encroaching darkness. "There's nothing fancy about those places. They push drugs and girls of any age. I've had friends go into those houses. They all got hooked on something."

"Junior's starting to sound like a problem," Adam pointed out, making a mental note.

The young woman paused and glanced back. "I thought you were helping him," she said.

"Why would you think that?" Holly asked.

"You've been getting rid of his competition. You've been helping him take over everything."

Adam said nothing. He could only growl.

"We didn't know that's what we were doing," Holly translated. "We were just looking for a little boy."

The young woman shrugged and continued up the stairs. "I didn't want to go into one of Junior's houses, and I couldn't afford to not have a job. One of my friends who had gotten out once told me about Abuela. So, I came here."

"Junior didn't mind you leaving?" Adam asked.

"He doesn't care. Girls come and go. As long as we don't go to the cops, he doesn't bother with us." She reached the second floor. This was a similar open plan, but with rooms sectioned off at the outer edge. Large tables dominated the center of the area, encircled with chairs. Each of the private offices had doors with large lettering indicating space for lawyers, councilors, or private meeting rooms. "Besides," the young woman said as she led Adam and Holly to the closed office at the furthest corner, "Nobody crosses Abuella."

"Why?" Adam asked cautiously.

The young woman stopped, as though caught by surprise. She blinked and her mouth opened and closed. "I…" she seemed unable to complete an answer, or even a thought relating to the question. Finally, she shrugged. "It just is."

The office to which the young woman led them was only labeled, "Abuela." The walls were glass, but smoked to obscure everything inside. The door opened just as the young woman reached for the handle, and she led them inside. Adam entered first, placing himself firmly in front of Holly, and looked around.

Abuela was an old woman, nothing more. Everything about her screamed "nice, helpless old lady." Her hair was more silver than grey, and lightly caught into a loose ponytail. She dressed simply, in unremarkable blue and white. She wore no jewelry or cosmetics. Her skin was unwrinkled and bore the weight of an entire lifetime, but without the weariness or damage such years typically brought with them. Her race could not be determined, as her coloring was too dark for the Americas, but too light for Africa. Her body was unbent, but also unremarkable. She did not have the firm allure of youth, but neither had her apparent years withered or bloated her body. She was unremarkable and unnoticeable.

She did not sit at a desk, but rather at some dedicated craft space. A low table was at her side, bearing colored paper, glue, scissors, paint and brushes, ribbon, and a variety of tiny tools. She sat in a simple chair, rocking back and forth as her hands danced before her. A line of wool or cotton trailed away from those hands, leading to a pile of colorful material at her side. Opposite of this, on Abuela's other side, was a low pile of knitted clothing. A new garment was manifesting in front of her, responding to the supposed old woman's mystical gestures and the flash of her knitting needles. Abuela was not looking at her new creation, though, instead focused on the new arrivals.

"Hello, Za'afiel," she said in a voice the held all the warmth of a grandmother's kitchen.

"I don't know you," the warrior replied wearily. Even with his greater senses numbed, still Adam could feel the pull of Abuela's voice. He caught himself leaning back, resisting the welcome enticement of the supposed old woman.

"But I know you," Abuela said, continuing her knitting. "I know all your kind, Fallen or not." She glanced at the young woman. Her eyes, Adam noted, were not any one color. They were the endless black of a moonless night, and yet they were also the warm brown of nurturing earth. They swam with the grey of storm clouds and flashed with blue lightning. They were the forest and the desert, the sea and the sky, the mountain and the valley. "Mary," Abuela said with a gentle, loving smile. "Would you go tell our guests that Za'afiel and his little friend are finally here."

"Yes, Abuela." The young woman left and closed the door.

"What is she?" Holly asked, taking a half step towards the supposed old woman. Her voice was hollow and her eyes nearly vacant.

Adam thrust an arm out, blocking his friend. "Knock it off," he growled at the creature that was certainly not an old woman. "I won't ask again."

Abuela smiled. "I apologize," she said, leaning back and continuing her knitting. "Even after all this time, I still forget the affect we have on Humans."

Holly blinked and shook her head, taking an instinctive step back and behind Adam. "What the hell?" she demanded in a voice of growing annoyance and indignation.

"She's a Daimon."

"A demon!?!" Holly gasped, pulling fully behind Adam.

"No. A Daimon." Adam emphasized the different sound of the word.

"'Demon' is a slur," Abuela sighed. "A corruption." Her changing eyes went up to Adam. "The Chorus want Humans to pull away from us and so implanted that word."

"You were warned," Adam growled. "All of you."

"Little context," Holly prompted, remaining mostly behind Adam.

"We're gods, little one," Abuela smiled.

Adam snorted.

"Well," the supposed old woman corrected, "we've been called gods. Worshipped as gods. We were meant to help Humanity, to guide you after you lost Paradise. We were supposed to help you develop rich civilizations. To learn science, art, music. To realize your potential."

"I thought angels weren't allowed to interfere," Holly said.

"They're not Angels," Adam said firmly.

"No, we were better," Abuela again smiled. "And worse. Angels were limited by the restriction of Free Will. Daimons were the other side of that particular coin. We were specifically meant to involve ourselves with Humans."

"Mythology," Holly deduced. "Zeus, Odin, Ra."

"And all the others," Abuela nodded. "Tengri, Wakea, Bochica, Shangdi. All of them and their offspring divided up the world and its peoples." She snorted then. "Of course, they wouldn't have gotten anything done if it wasn't for us."

"Us?"

"Isis, Nana Buluku, Izanami, Cybele, Durga. Without us, your civilizations would have never gotten started."

"I don't understand," Holly admitted.

"After Eden," Adam explained, his eyes locked on Abuela, "Humanity needed guidance. We couldn't do it because of Free Will. The Daimons were supposed to fill in that gap. They were supposed to help you get started and to guide you through your earliest ages." His voice went flat, then. "But too many of them were corrupted."

"Humans started worshipping us. Many of my associates developed an affection for… ritual."

"And sacrifice," Adam's voice had become as hard as granite.

Abuela sighed and nodded. "A few," she conceded. "And so, the censure."

"Censure?"

"Egypt." Adam said flatly. "The plagues. A message to all their kind to back off."

"And we did," Abuela noted. "Most of us."

"Yeah, most. But some needed a personal visit. They either got the message, or they were cast down."

"Yes," Abuela's shifting eyes locked with Adam's. "Most. There's always a few holdouts, however. And, of course, my fellows and I can't help but continue our rolls as Humanity's guides." She glanced towards the door. "Speaking of."

The door opened and Kiliahoté entered. He still looked as falsely-innocent as always. Nondescript jeans and a dress shirt wrapped his thin, unremarkable frame. His flesh and eyes still presented themselves as one of the indigenous peoples of this land, though lacking the natural weathering of a Human. His dark hair was not bound as he usually kept it, appearing neat and organized in his pretense of being a museum curator. Instead, Kiliahoté looked just slightly harried and tired.

"Coyote," Adam almost sneered. Whereas Abuela took pains to slide from memory, to encourage comfort and trust, Kiliahoté only ever drew suspicion. For all his efforts at blending in, at disappearing from notice, no Trickster could avoid notice for long.

"Za'afiel," Kiliahoté smiled. "Still causing Destruction everywhere you go?"

"Still causing Chaos?"

The Trickster shrugged. "We all must follow our natures." He gestured behind him and a young boy stepped forward. "I believe you've met my young friend."

"Hello, brother," the boy said.

Adam stumbled back, nearly falling. "Haziel!"

The boy appeared innocent and common. Unremarkable eyes and hair. Bland features that would go unnoticed by any Human. A quiet voice that was forgotten the moment it went silent. All of this worked only on mortal minds, however. Even with his blunted senses, still Adam could not help but recognize another of the Fallen.

"Not Haziel," the boy corrected with a sad shake of his head. "Not anymore. Any more than you're truly Za'afiel. Even as you're now Adam, so I'm now Peter."

Adam ran up and knelt before Haziel. "When did you Fall?" the warrior demanded. "How?"

"I didn't," the boy replied. "Not exactly. I was chosen by the Choir. I was supposed to be safe, here on Earth."

"Safe from what?" Adam demanded. "Chosen for what?"

The boy glanced up at Kiliahoté who shrugged. He then looked to Abuela, who nodded. He then sighed and looked down. "I'm one of the Ten."

Adam fell, hitting the floor and almost unconsciously scrambling backwards, away from the boy and the power he held.

Holly stepped forward, looking from Adam to Peter in confusion. "What is it?" she demanded of her partner. "What the hell is wrong with you?"

"It's not his fault, Ms. MacAllister," Peter said gently. He looked from her to Adam and back. "We all react like that, since the Rebellion."

"Your bible begins with mention of how the world was created with a spoken Word, isn't that right, Ms. MacAllister?" Abuela asked.

Holly nodded.

"The Word was the point of the Rebellion," Kilihoté said. "The Tetragrammaton. It's what Lucifer and Orobas and all the others were after. The power of creation."

"To make, remake, or unmake anything, into anything." Abuela sighed, briefly pausing her knitting and rubbing her inconstant eyes. "After the failed Rebellion, the Word was broken into Ten Pieces and scattered." The supposed old woman resumed her weaving. "Only once in all Human time have they been regathered into one body. Since then, they've remained separated, and for good reason." She turned her gaze to Adam, her shifting eyes for once holding on hard black. "Za'afiel," she said in an equally-unflinching voice. "Lilith is gathering the Pieces."

"What!?!" Adam was on his feet, his fists clenched hard. "How the Hell long has this been going on!?!"

"Years," Abuela replied.

"Centuries," Kilihoté corrected. He and Adam locked gazes. "She's been at it since the Age of Sail, when she could start moving around faster. You Angels, your Chorus, has been trying to keep it secret. Me and my kind have spent all this time trying to slow her down, to keep the pieces moving. But she's winning. She's almost got them all."

"All but one," Peter added.

"Tricksters," Adam sneered, making the word an insult. "Why not just stop the bitch?" He looked to Abuela. "Isn't that your damned job? You're supposed to guide Humanity! To stop shit like this before it becomes a problem! Why the Hell have you let this go on for so long?"

"Because she's Lilith," Abuela replied darkly. "The first. The original. The source. She has an army of her children and power unlike anything else."

"Not to mention that we tried," Kiliahoté added grimly.

Adam glanced at him and the Trickster shrugged. "Yokohama, 1923," he said. "Over a hundred of us gathered to confront her, to try and stop her. The result…"

"Fire," Peter whispered. "Earthquake. Tsunami. 140,000 dead." He looked to Adam. "That's when I became involved. I was sent to offer mercy to the suffering. I found the previous bearer of this Piece in the rubble. Lilith was nearby and closing."

"We were still trying to keep her distracted," Kiliahoté added. "Unsuccessfully."

"Time was short," Peter continued. "The Chorus decided to change tactics."

"Normally," Abuela said, resuming her knitting, "when one bearer dies, the Piece transfers to another newborn Human. This is how Lilith has been gathering them. She would locate a bearer and capture him. She would produce another child and, in the moment of birth, kill the bearer. The Piece would transfer to her newborn. That was likely her plan in Yokohama."

"I transubstantiated," Peter said. "In the instant the bearer was released, I took Human form. The Piece transferred to me, and I've been carrying it ever since."

"And we've been hiding him," Kiliahoté added. "Keeping him on the move and out of sight."

"That's not a winning strategy," Holly noted.

"A delay, at best," Adam agreed.

"We know," Abuela sighed. She glanced at Kiliahoté. "So we came up with a new strategy."

"We needed someone with the power and skill to face Lilith and her children. We needed someone who could cut down those false-bearers and release the Tetragrammaton back into world." The Trickster grimaced. "We needed…"

"An Angel of Destruction," Holly finished. She stepped away from Peter and stood beside Adam. She slipped one of her tiny hands into his, in defiance of his stated aversion to her doing so. Unlike the other times, Adam did not shrink away. He said nothing as the weight of their manipulation began pressing down on him.

"But a Fallen one," Abuela corrected. "No Angel could intervene, since it involves Humans. The Lilim, Lilith's bastards, despite being evil and nearly immortal, are still protected by Free Will. An Angel cannot intervene."

"But a Fallen can," Kiliahoté pointed out. "We considered trying to enlist your brother, Chezef."

"He wouldn't help," Adam said numbly. "He wouldn't care."

"That was the key ingredient," Abuela agreed. "We needed an Angel of Destruction who cared enough to help. None of your Choir cares. You were all created for that one purpose. None of them spend any time with Humans; none of them have any investment in this world. You are the outlier, Za'afiel. You always have been."

"We've been watching you for centuries," Kiliahoté admitted. "We've noticed how you've been… changing."

"You alone," Abuela said, "care. You alone have tried to help Humans. We've noticed you repeatedly enlisting the Watchers to attempt preventions. You've encouraged warnings, last chances. Anything within your power to spare Humans the suffering you brought. You are the only one who had the skill and power to stop Lilith, but who also had compassion enough to stop her."

The supposed old woman's inconstant eyes shifted to Holly. "Consider how you two first met," she pointed out. "You did not have to help her, Za'afiel. You were under no obligation."

"In fact," Kiliahoté added," helping her only caused you more problems, as you suspected would happen. And yet, you still helped her."

"I was guilted into it," Adam huffed.

Abuela smiled. "Yes, by your bartender. And she needed so much effort to convince you." The Trickster in the shape of an innocent old woman shook her head, still knitting, still weaving her desired reality. "You were never like the other Angels of Destruction, Za'afiel. They obey without question. They destroy, inflict misery, and return to your Silver City awaiting orders to do so again. Only you questioned your duty. Only you tried working around the mandates of the Chorus. You were exactly what we needed to defeat Lilith."

"But," Kiliahoté continued, "you were an Angel. Limited by Free Will. So we watched, and waited."

"And then there was London," Abuela noted gently. "And your trial."

"It was you," Holly nearly whispered, her already pale face losing every trace of color.

Adam looked down at her, and those large, dark eyes glanced up at him, becoming pools of shared emotion, of outrage and sadness and realization. "It was them," she breathed again. "They're the reason you're here."

The warrior's eyes, not swimming pools of feeling like Holly's, were instead granite. Those unforgiving, unrelenting stones went from one Trickster to another and back. "It was you," he said. His voice was level, but the implication of his words, his tone, his entire existence, promised vengeance. "You did this."

Both Tricksters were silent for a moment. They glanced at each other, obviously afraid. They had poked at the wolf, steering him, prodding at him, and now the monster's gaze was solely upon them. Abuela said, "That *Drest-Vidar* wizard you killed was the one who-"

"DON'T GIVE ME THAT!" Adam roared. Still, his rage was held, if only just, but Holly's small hand, engulfed in the warrior's. He was only dimly aware of it, of her presence beside him. He did not know, nor understand why he held on, did not shake himself free of her and unleash his justified fury on these Tricksters. His other fist was clenched so hard that, had he picked up a diamond, he would have crushed it to powder. Somehow, though, the hand that held hers remained gentle.

Kiliahoté and Abuela glanced again at each other. "We may have made a few suggestions."

Adam said nothing. He could say nothing. Too much hatred was writhing in his mind. Too much wrath was burning up from his heart, searing the back of his throat. The warrior knew the remedy for what he felt. He knew the violence that would soothe him, return to him the welcome cold of unfeeling. Still, he had that tiny anchor in his hand that would not let him be free.

"Za'afiel," Peter's small voice said then. "Adam. I didn't want this either." He gestured to the boy's body in which he was imprisoned. "Wearing this form for over a century? Tasked with protecting one of the Ten Pieces of the Tetragrammaton? Burdened with preventing Lilith from gaining them all? I didn't want any of this. But it has to be done."

His youthful eyes, doorways that shone from behind with all the eternal compassion, mercy, and forgiveness that had been his duty. "You didn't want to protect that girl in London, but you knew it had to be done. You didn't want… what happened to her, but it was forced. You didn't want to continue unleashing Destruction upon Humanity. You didn't want to kill that *Drest-Vidar* wizard or face his family. You didn't want to help Ms. MacAllister. But all this happened. We are where we are. Mine is the only Piece left."

"Lilith has the other nine," Kiliahoté reminded. "Peter's is all that remains. We, me and my kind, have tried for centuries to keep them safe." He looked to Peter and shook his head. "But we failed. We're not protectors. We're not warriors. Our tricks can only do so much.

"I got Peter free of Agarés, but he got captured again by those criminals working for Orobas," Kiliahoté admitted. "They're competing with each other to give Lilith the last Piece, to earn her favor. Between those two forces, there was only so much we could do. It took you," he gestured to both Adam and Holly, "both of you, to free him again." The Trickster nodded at Abuela. "We're at the limits of what we can do. We need help. We need someone who gives a damn if Lilith gains the power to remake Creation to her pleasure."

"Did you make a suggestion to summon Chezef?" Holly asked suddenly.

Both of the Tricksters blinked in surprise. "What?" Kiliahote started.

"Did you arrange for him to be here," the woman repeated again. She glanced up at Adam. "We stopped. We were taking a few days off. We were going to keep looking for the boy, but not right away. But then…"

"But then my brother arrived in town," Adam growled, following his partner's line of thought. "That got us moving again." He turned once more to burn the Tricksters with his hate. "Well?"

"We didn't summon him," Abuela insisted.

Kiliahoté raised his hands defensively, "or make any suggestions to do so."

"He is our backup, though," the supposed old woman admitted. "If you refuse us, Za'afiel, or if you fail, we'll have to plea to Chezef for help. We were keeping him nearby, up in Dallas, until we could be certain that you would help. We were hoping, with enough time, you would be ready. We hadn't planned on bringing you and Peter together yet, but..."

"Orobas is the one who called you brother in early," Kiliahoté added. "We've run out of time."

"He knew," Holly mused, almost to himself. "He's manipulated so much of what happens in Meropis County. He knows about you two, right?"

The Tricksters grimly nodded.

"He's probably kept track of what you've been doing. He knew you had Chezef in Dallas." She locked eyes again with Adam. "He got Peter away from Kiliahoté before, he could do it again. But he needed us... he needed you distracted."

All was silent then. Every violent instinct in Adam's unwanted soul screamed at him to either turn away these liars and manipulators, or to exact bloody vengeance. The warrior thrashed against what had been done to him, yearned to turn his back forever. All that held him was one tiny, immovable object.

"I've arranged for Chezef to be distracted," Abuela said. "But I can't keep him away forever. He doesn't know about Peter and Lilith's involvement."

"And, as you said," Kiliahoté added. "He probably wouldn't care." The Coyote looked down at Peter sadly. "We don't know what to do, Za'afiel. The last Piece must be protected. Lilith must be stopped. Orobas has sold himself to her. He wants, more than anything, the power and respect the Mother of Hell can provide, if she acquires the entire Tetragrammaton. He'll risk much, perhaps everything, to get the last Piece to her. He's even willing to risk Chezef destroying this town."

Holly pulled slightly on Adam's hand, drawing his ear down. "Everything else aside," she said gently, "all the tricks and the lies and whatever else. All the cosmic doom and family problems. Everything about this is second."

"What's first?" Adam asked.

Holly glanced at Peter. "He asked for help. He asked, and only we're able to help him."

Adam straightened and sighed. He looked at Peter, at the immature prison into which his friend, his comrade, and his brother had been condemned. The warrior relented and the fire burning its way up was suddenly quenched. Adam shook his head and said, “Damn.”

11

"Do we have anything like a plan?" Holly asked.

Adam was already moving. He knelt in front of Peter, the little brother he had not seen in over a century. "If I'd known," he said gently. "If the Chorus had told me what was happening, all those years ago…"

Peter put a hand on his older brother's broad shoulder. "You know now."

Adam nodded. He glanced back and gestured Holly forward. "This is my friend. I trust her. No matter what happens, stay with her. Do what she says."

Peter looked up at Holly, who smiled at him. The Fallen imprisoned in a boy's body hesitantly smiled back at her.

Adam stood and squared his shoulders, staring hard at Kiliahoté. "When this is over, you and me are going to have a talk."

The Coyote looked as though he might say something, but whatever sarcastic wit that was about to tumble out died on his tongue. He only took a step back and nodded.

Adam sighed and cracked his neck. "I assume those cops outside are loyal to Orobas?" he said to Abuela.

The supposed old woman nodded. "They're here to get Peter back."

"Alight, that's the immediate problem." The warrior glanced at Holly. "I'll get their attention. You take Haziel…" he looked at the boy. "You take Peter out back. I'll draw all the cops to me. You two use that to escape. Get the Beast and ride to the Twins' ranch. They've got enough private security to hold off Orobas' people, and they've got the resources to get him out of Disanté."

"What about you?" Holly asked.

Adam shrugged, starting to work the stiffness out of his still-healing body. "After I deal with the cops, I'll lead Chezef away." The warrior looked again to Abuela. "Is there any kind of time limit, here?"

The Trickster playing at being an innocent old woman shook her head. "Lilith has been seeking the Pieces for centuries."

Adam exhaled explosively. "Fine. Make sure whatever people you have in this building are safe." He started moving through the door. "It's about to get real collateral around here."

"We're not just going to abandon you to the cops!" Holly insisted, taking Peter's hand and following behind Adam.

"You'll do as your told," the warrior grunted, heading for the stairs. "Keep Peter and that last Piece safe. Get him to the Twins. They've got enough contacts to hide him."

"How is that a plan?" Holly demanded. "That's no better than what they were doing!" she jabbed a thumb back at the Tricksters.

"It's all we can do in the short term. I get Orobas' people off you. I keep Chezef away from you. After that…"

"What 'after that'?" Holly rushed ahead and stood in front of Adam, her arms outstretched. "Chezef kicked your ass up one side and down the other! He won't stop!"

Adam put his hands on her tiny shoulders. "But you'll be safe." He glanced at Peter. "You both will. Our job here isn't to win some great victory. It's to win one more day, to keep the Piece out of Lilith's hands. Now, do as I say."

Holly paused a moment, and then stood aside. "Okay," she said submissively.

Adam eyed her suspiciously. "Don't try to thwart me, woman," he growled.

His partner looked up at him with enormous eyes that swam with utter sincerity and obedience. Adam did not trust those lying eyes. He held up a finger, ready to unleash a barrage of hateful, dominating curses and commands. Holly only tilted her head slightly, obviously ready with a wall of female inflexibility. Adam let his hand fall, turning to walk down the stairs, repeatedly muttering, "Damn," though frustrated, clenched teeth.

Adam reached the main floor and kept moving towards the door. He made note of the back door, leading to the free clinic, and the administrative station to his left with its thick wooden shelves. The warrior did not create a plan in his mind, but rather let his centuries of experience take over. The world went calm. His emotions, so often alien and unwanted, drifted away. He breathed in the cold, stale air while opening his limited mortal senses. He clenched and released each of his muscle groups in sequence, making them ready.

His hands were stiff, slow in response. The burns on his left hand had healed as much as they would. The skin was roughly-textured and discolored. He had lost some of his sensation there, and his grip was slightly weaker. The physical therapy Holly, and later Candace, had insisted upon had restored much of his dexterity, but not all.

His right hand had also healed as much as it likely would. The center of his palm still bore the divot, the indentation of where René Casimir had stabbed him with the Gault Spear. Like his left, the right hand had endured the mandated physical therapy and regained much of its utility. Much, but not all. The fingers no longer fully clenched or released. The doctors had done what they could, and Adam's own Fallen anatomy had also contributed, but there were limits. he would never again have full utility.

He encouraged blood to flow out, through his limbs. The warrior paused a moment at the large front doors, adjusting his long white leather coat. His body would not naturally age. The Fallen were meant to be frozen. Part of their punishment was to endure while they watched Humans age and die. No, they did not grow old, but they did accumulate damage. Adam's body was slowing. The many battles, many victories and defeats, were beginning to accumulate. And here he was, diving into the fire once more. The warrior did not fight the smile breaching onto his weathered, scarred face.

Adam exited through the front doors, pausing a moment. The vehicles were still parked, still awaiting orders. *As usual,* he thought darkly, *Orobas is flip-flopping around possible decisions.* The Fallen Watcher would be wrestling through scenarios and strategies for hours, Adam knew. He was brilliant, but that brilliance was as much a problem as an asset.

Time to force the issue.

Adam walked up to one of the parked vehicles, the same one he had looked in when he and Holly had first arrived. He stood in front, looking in once more, and watched for a moment as the cop inside was staring at him and talking urgently into a radio. The warrior then half-turned and rammed his elbow through the window. The men inside cursed and recoiled from the unexpected assault. Adam did not give them time to adapt, however, instead reaching in and grabbing the small canister he had noted attached to the cop's vest. Adam did not extract the entire grenade, though, but only the safety clip and pin.

"FUCK!" came a growing chorus from inside the vehicle. "FUCK! FUCK! FUCK!" More curses joined in the song as colorful smoke began pouring out from the vehicle. Everyone inside exited, coughing and swearing and promising retribution. Adam was already back inside the shelter.

Muffled commands laced with curses filled the air, coming from mouths and radios. Two sets of men formed on either side of the building, with jerky hand-motions trying to coordinate their effort.

They're new, the warrior mused. *Or, at least unfamiliar with each other.*

The two groups held their position, just beyond the large windows on either side of the double doors. They were waiting. Sounds from beyond the free clinic revealed for what they were waiting. A third team, then, meant to enter from behind. Time passed. Foolishly, as this gave the deadly warrior inside more time to prepare.

Finally, one of the front teams, the one to the right of the doors, moved forward. They tried for silence, whispering hoarsely to one another with yet more confused hand gestures. That breach team reached the doors and paused again. One of their number came forward carrying a massive cylinder. This man reached the front and braced himself, rearing back with his battering ram.

In the instant the ram would have touched the door, Adam opened it.

"Shit!" The cop holding the ram was dedicated to the movement, but not overly so. He was solid on his feet and could have stopped, except that, in the same instant he opened the door, Adam grabbed the ram by its forward handle and heaved. "OH, FUCK!" the cop screamed as he was pulled into the darkness within. Adam dove forward, while the man was still airborne, grabbing onto his back and slamming him into the unyielding floor. The warrior also, in the same movement, grabbed a small cylinder from the cop's belt. Adam released the safety clip and pulled the pin. He hit the ground with his first target and rolled, tossing the grenade back out the front door.

"FUCK!" was the responding chorus. Men on either side of the building dove for cover they could not find. Their world exploded into a screaming white void. They swore and shook their heads, desperately trying to clear their eyes and ears.

"Motherfucker!" one of them snarled, picking up his shotgun and lunging inside.

Adam shot him with the first cop's stun gun. The warrior had meant to hit his target in the armored chest, just above the heart. This would, he thought, minimize the damage. However, Adam was never a good aim.

"Dumbass future-crap!" the warrior barked in irritation as the twin wires lanced out and struck the oncoming cop in the groin. The man tried to scream, but his entire body was locked in a contortion, a mockery of frozen dance. Only a pitiful, squeaking, chittering grunt escaped the cop's lips as he seemed to stand rigid for a moment, and then fall into a pool of spasms and urine.

"Screw it," Adam grunted, drawing his knife. He rolled forward just as the last two men of the breaching team came through the door. He impacted the legs of the man on the right, sending him cursing to the floor. Adam was instantly on his feet, spinning and deflecting the left-side man's shotgun even as it fired. To his credit, the target realized how useless an extended barrel was in such close quarters and dropped the weapon, his hand going to the pistol on his hip. Adam was too fast, though, grabbing that arm with his free hand. Normally, he would have stripped the firearm, but his hand was slow in responding to his need. Instead, the warrior could only push it aside, stabbing into the inside of that elbow. The target screamed, even as his attacker pivoted, still holding the now-useless arm, and threw the man over his shoulder, into his partner who had been trying to rise.

Adam darted forward. The last man of the breaching team was trying to call for help through his radio even as he tried to regain his feet. Both the movement and the call were cut off, as the warrior brought his booted foot up and drove down onto the cop's face. His feet, at least, were still fully functional.

Shouts came from outside as the second team rushed for the door. This put them directly in front of one of the large windows resting on either side of the building's main entrance. Adam grabbed the pistol from one of the downed cops and fired it. He did not bother trying for accuracy, instead pointing the idiot machine well above anyone's head. He fired again and again, high and through the window and causing the incoming team to hit the ground. Adam emptied the clip and tossed away the useless metal thing while he ran for the administrative alcove and its controls.

The second team recovered enough to return fire. Their shots tore into the building, shredding furniture, books, teaching boards, games, and all the other threats to modern security. They fired blindly, uncaring of what they hit. The last of the teams, the one that was already moving through the free clinic and towards the main room, swore. The sounds of impacts came through those rear doors as the men obviously sought cover, yelling at their compatriots to stop shooting at them.

Adam waited.

The second team breached the doors. They did so in a much better-coordinated movement that had the first team. The four men moved in unison, the first two swinging wide to either side of the door, while the second two held the center. Everything inside was quiet and dark. "Nods," came a too-loud whisper. In response, the four men reached up to the things attached to their helmets. These machines were swung down, across their eyes.

Adam turned on the lights.

"Ah!"

"Shit!"

"Fuck!"

Adam lunged in. He batted aside one shotgun barrel and grabbed another with his stiff grip. He planted his shoulder into the weapon's owner and flipped the screaming man end over end. The warrior then used the captured shotgun like a club, the unfeeling fingers slipping out of the trigger well. Adapting, Adam rammed the stock of his borrowed shotgun into one cop's unprotected middle before jabbing the barrel into another's crotch. Adam grabbed that barrel in both hands and swung the shotgun in wide arcs, impacting one chin after another. *Killing these assholes would be a Hell of a lot easier*, he thought as he continued incapacitating the attackers, almost hearing another of Holly's lectures on lethal violence.

The second team was down. Men were lying on the ground all around Adam, some moaning, some quiet. Some of them squirmed in pain, holding broken bones or shattered teeth, others cradling abused bits of their bodies. Another two teams were already approaching from the other side of the street. Adam shook his head at this division of forces and glanced towards the back and the free clinic.

"Oh, you sneaky little bastards!" the warrior growled.

The team that had tried the obvious tactic of entering from the rear were not moving to engage him, as the warrior had assumed they would. Instead, the six men were moving along the rear wall, towards the staircase.

Adam charged.

One of the cops glanced back. He was not carrying another shotgun, but rather a short-barreled rifle. He pivoted and fired, forcing Adam to seek cover against one of the large pillars holding the upper floors in place.

"Keep going!" one of the cops said as he began climbing the stairs. "You two kill him!"

Two of the cops oriented towards Adam as the rest continued onto the stairs. The two assigned to kill him approached the warrior wearily, weapons raised and steady. From behind the pilar, Adam noted the approach of the remaining outside men. *No choice now*, he grimly realized, forcing his grip to tighten as much as it could onto his knife.

The two cops approaching from the back moved to either side of the pillar, intending to attack from both directions. Adam did not wait. He lunged forward, grabbing the man's barrel and moving it the fraction of an inch needed to avoid his head. A shot rang out and the cop screamed. Adam had used his other hand to slash with his blade, opening the man's stomach. The second cop fired into Adam's back, but the white leather coat stopped the bullets. Pain exploded in his tiring body. White hot pain that seared from his spine, up into his brain. The coat prevented any penetration, it negated the mot lethal effects of the shotgun blast, but still the impact remained. The cop who had shot Adam in the back paused, clearly taken aback by what he saw. His shot should have caused the warrior's entire torso to explode in a shower of gore; instead, Adam roared his pain-filled outrage and spun, confronting his attacker. This instant of uncertainty gave the warrior the half-second needed to close the distance. He wrapped his arm around the cop's shotgun and brough his other elbow up and then down onto the man's arm, knocking aside the weapon. Adam then turned his blade so that it was pointing down and jabbed his knife into the man's neck.

The warrior took a handful of precious moments to retrieve two more grenades from the dead and dying men, tossing them out to slow the approaching reinforcements. Adam did not wait to see what affect the flash and the bang had on the men, instead sprinting for the stairs. The cop furthest down, the last to try and make the climb, felt Death's approach and turned, but had time only to grunt as Adam impacted the man, sending him to the stairs where the warrior landed several vicious kicks that shattered ribs and brought a torrent of blood from the man's mouth and nose.

Adam threw his knife and the next man up, sending the blade into the narrow gap within the man's shoulder. The cop screamed and felt to his knees, dropping his weapon and cradling the knife handle protruding from his body.

The warrior glanced up. He jumped and rebounded off the wall to plant a foot on the staircase. He then used the growing momentum to launch upwards, grabbing the next flight of stairs with stiffening fingers and hauling himself up. Adam shoved his shoulder into one of the cops, sending the man grunting and tumbling down the stairs. He then turned and spun his arm in a wide circle, deflecting the orienting rifle away. The warrior spotted a sheathed knife in the man's boot, and grabbed it, pulling up only to stab down, opening the many veins behind the man's knee.

Adam grabbed the man's pistol and marched up the remaining stairs. He fired high again, forcing the remaining cops there to dive to the ground. The warrior sprinted forward and jammed his knee up into one face, only to use the rebounding force to drive that boot into the jaw of the last man.

Shouting, cursing voices came from below. The reinforcements on the ground floor had recovered and were entering the building.

Adam turned, and was met with a baton across his chin. The warrior allowed the energy of the strike to spin him completely. He released control of his body for a moment, allowing instinct, experience, and training to take over. His torso crouched and pivoted on one foot, the other lancing out and knocking his attacker back a few steps. Snarling through the stars obscuring his vision, Adam darted forward and reached out with both his arms. He grabbed the cop behind the knee and shoved his broad shoulder up into the man, knocking him backwards. The cop stumbled, but did not fall, twisting away from Adam, but losing his weapon. Both men settled into fighting stances, knees slightly bent and fists up. Adam darted forward and jabbed again and again with his loose fists, driving his opponent back. The cop had his own arms up in a good defensive posture, blocking or absorbing each of Adam's strikes. The warrior kept driving, kept pushing forward with his fists, until the target was back at the stairs. Adam then made several rapid, wide swings of his arms to draw the defender up, before landing a solid kick to the man's middle, sending him tumbling down the steps.

Adam lunged forward, grabbing the cop's helmet and pulling the face up, exposing it. The warrior punched, again and again, shattering the man's face. By the time Adam let go of the man, little was left but bloody meat.

There was a busing in Adam's pocket. He retrieved the idiot box Holly had insisted he carry, looking at the tiny screen.

WE'RE SAFE! GET OUT!

Adam, panting and bleeding, glanced towards the front doors. Several more cops were pouring in. Their weapons were raised and the murderous intent was clear. The warrior glanced back up the stairs at the dead-end of offices there. He then looked over his shoulder.

Screw it.

The warrior spat a thickening wad of blood and turned, throwing himself through the large window at the back of the stairwell. "Oh shit!" was all he had time to say before crashing into a large dumpster in the alley below.

Coughing blood and cursing the Tricksters, Adam tumbled out of the dumpster. Blinding amber light filled the alley and the roar of the Beast shattered the cold night. "Will you get on!?!" Holly demanded.

Adam looked up through what he realized was a blackening eye and a bleeding nose. Holly was astride the Beast, her short arms barely reaching the extended handlebars. Peter was sitting behind her, his youthful-appearing arms wrapped tightly around the girl's tiny waist.

"Move," Adam commanded and demanded.

"Just get on!" his imperious partner snapped, jabbing a thumb to the now-extended passenger seat behind her.

"I am not riding bitch!" the warrior thundered.

Flashing lights behind them and the squeal of approaching cops ended the debate. "Bitch or body bag!" Holly declared.

Adam shook his head and climbed on, furiously wrapping his arms around Peter and Holly. "Go! Go! Go!" And the Beast roared into the night.

12

"Why are we stopping here?" Holly asked as she pulled the Beast in front of their apartment building.

Adam dismounted with relief. "Get your things," he grumbled, taking the time to set his broken nose back into place. "Pack light. We're leaving town."

Holly nodded and dismounted, affectionately stroking the Beast's instrument display. "Good boy," she whispered to him and the bike purred contentedly.

"Hurry the Hell up!" Adam barked.

Peter caught up to the fuming, sore warrior. "Where will we go?" the boy asked.

"Away," Adam growled. "Out of town. We get away, then we have time to plan. First, away."

Holly caught up as the warrior reached the metal gate and held it open. "Do you think we'll be able to come back?" she asked, easily walking under Adam's arm. As she walked, she almost instinctively took Peter's hand.

"No," the warrior grimaced, following them into the courtyard. "Or, not likely, anyway." The complex was as dark and silent as the rest of Disanté had become. Few lights shown down from the many apartments. There was no music, no laughter. The complex had, for the past few weeks, joined in the general cheerful attitude Adam and Holly had noted in the town. Festive lights had been hung, wreaths adorned doors, holiday music occasionally drifted through windows. Many of their neighbors had even brought in Christmas trees, though few of these were real. Holly had joined in with this increasingly-festive mood, stringing multi-colored lights across their apartment, hanging a bizarre mixture of traditional and adorably-modern decorations, and producing batch after batch of seasonal cookies.

Adam grudgingly allowed the decorating, as he had no choice, but silently welcomed the plethora of treats.

"What about all our stuff?" Holly asked as they reached the stairs that led up to their apartment.

"Your stuff, you mean?" Adam replied sourly. "Leave it. We're traveling light."

Something in the back of the warrior's mind alerted him, a fraction of a second before the explosion. Some instinct, some remnant of his Celestial senses, had his body moving even as his thoughts struggled to process what was happening. He grabbed Holly and Peter, enfolding them in his impenetrable white leather coat, and dove for the pool as the world above them erupted in fire and debris.

The pool was yet another of the strange, subtle changes affecting Adam's world. For the months he had lived in this complex before Holly's intrusion into his life, the pool had only ever been, at best, half-filled. The property manager never had it cleaned or serviced. More often than not, local wildlife made greater use than those who dwelled within the surrounding apartments. None of the residents had made much of the pool; everyone either did not care or accepted the greedy indifference of their landlord.

But then, Holly had joined their small world. Within weeks of moving into Adam's apartment, she had begun a steady campaign of artfully-adorable pleading, indignant cajoling, and unending badgering on not only the property manager, but the company that owned the complex. Adam had noticed her efforts but shrugged them off, assuming they would fail. To the surprise of everyone in their community, most especially her faithless partner, Holly had won.

Days after Halloween, the pool had been drained, cleaned, repaired, and refilled, just in time for the weather to cool. Workmen had surrounded the center courtyard of the apartment complex for over a week. By the time their labor was done, the pool looked as though it were brand new. Every resident had joined with Adam and Holly in their silent observation of the new, completed pool. They had, as a small community, encircled it and stared, marveling.

Holly, beaming in her victory, had declared that they would have a pool party, just as soon as the weather warmed enough. To Adam's great surprise, none of the residents, himself included, raised any objection, and every time the girl walked through the complex, some passing resident would remind her of the promised party and make suggestions for its implementation.

Instead of Holly's party, though, the first use of the pool was as shelter from the fiery destruction of the apartment complex.

Adam surged to the surface, carrying Holly and Peter with him. They emerged, sucking in air. The warrior took half a moment to glance down. He had instinctively grabbed Holly, as he had done many times before, to protect her from whatever his instincts had detected by enfolding her in his impenetrable white leather coat. She, in turn, had grabbed Peter and pulled him close to her, enfolding the Fallen Cherub even as Adam enfolded her. To the warrior's relief, other than being now-drenched in freezing water, the two were untouched by fire or debris.

The warrior, however, had several new cuts to the back of his head.

"MOVE!" he thundered, bringing them into the shallow end of the pool with only a few strokes of one powerful arm and kicks of his muscled legs.

The apartments were doomed. The warrior knew this in an instant. Of the four sides to the complex, the one containing Adam and Holly's home was already burning rubble. The explosion had destroyed nearly the entire wing. Wreckage, wood, concrete, furniture, and personal belongings, had been hurled far into the uncaring clouds. The apartments opposite the destroyed wing had been assaulted with a torrent of shrapnel. The fire was already spreading, helped by secondary explosions as the various gas lines ignited.

"MOVE!" Adam roared again, nearly hauling Holly and Peter out of the pool and towards the relative safety of the closed iron gate, which in turn led to the street. The warrior ignored the flaming debris raining down all around them. He barely registered when something aflame struck his back. He only considered the safety of Holly and Peter. They remained covered in the large folds of his white leather coat and his own heavy frame. Adam did not pause in their mad flight, not even against the hard iron of the front gate. Instead, he lowered his shoulder and rammed his full weight against it. The portal offered only a single, started squeak as he barreled through it with those he had promised to protect.

The Beast, who had probably only just returned to his storage unit, was already on the street, engine growling in concern. Adam ran to the motorcycle and firmly placed Holly and Peter upon the saddle. "Protect them!" he barked and turned back to the burning building.

The warrior rushed back into flames, trusting to his white leather coat and his own indifference towards his unwanted mortal flesh. He ignored the unmoving bodies and the chunks of burned meat. He opened his mundane senses, pushing through the roar of fire and explosion and tragedy. Screams, sobbing, and pitiful cries for help became his sole focus. Adam lunged through a door and grabbed an old man, ignoring his sounds of fear and pain, instead wrapping the elderly Human in his coat and rushing him outside. He placed this first recovered resident on the ground in front of Holly, saying nothing as he turned back. Adam trusted her to help however was possible.

The warrior lunged back into the inferno. Small, fading sounds drew him to the left. A door was a wall of fire, so he leapt through the accompanying window instead. Rolling back to his feet, Adam spotted a single, young mother and her two children, cowering against a far wall. This family he picked up and, just as with the old man, engulfed them in his coat. The flaming door was destroyed with one furious kick, and the mother and her children were left with Holly.

Adam had never bothered learning the names of his neighbors. He never bothered being friendly with them. In the time of his sole occupation, the warrior had been indifferent to the other mortals living in proximity to him. Even after Holly's introduction, and her mandated neighborliness, still Adam made only the barest of nods towards familiarity. This effort most often took the form of grunts and acknowledging nods when one of them said hello.

None of that mattered now, however. Adam's desired isolation, his attempts at self-destruction, his indifference for his dwelling or its other inhabitants. None of that mattered. Holly's enforced cordiality did not matter either. Adam's mind was blank as he worked. His sullen misery at being imprisoned within mortal flesh retreated. The warrior's constant need for violence, too, faded into the background. He did not feel his seething intolerance for Human folly, the ache to administer the doom they seemed so determined to bring upon themselves. He felt none of this in that unending moment.

For a few, scattered moments, when conscious thought intruded upon his work, Adam tried to understand what he was feeling as he pulled one survivor after the next from the flaming wreckage of their home. He was not angry, for he understood anger very well. He was not afraid, despite all the burning reasons to be. The warrior was not anxious or tired or worried.

He was none of those things. As he grabbed a burning wooden beam and heaved it off a father, letting his wife and children pull him free, Adam wondered if this wasn't some remnant of the empty fury that had once defined Za'afiel. Every time his duty to the Chorus had required acts of cruel Destruction, the Angel had retreated into that safe void of unfeeling. That had been what preserved his sanity in the unending centuries of blood and horror. But this was not that.

The three stairways were useless by the time Adam had cleared the first floor and was ready to work on the second. So, the warrior used the short iron fence surrounding the pool to vault up, grabbing the railing lining the second story and heaved himself up. Even the stiff inflexibility of his hands seemed to retreat against this newest crisis. His limbs obeyed his commands, responding to his need with renewed dexterity. As Adam went from apartment to apartment, calling for survivors to make themselves known, the warrior came to a realization.

Holly would say he was happy, that he was enjoying the crisis. But she would have been wrong, Adam realized. This was not happiness, though he had little basis for comparison. He was not enjoying the suffering of his neighbors. No, he had seen this reaction from time to time in the aftermath of his visits to Humans. When he had brought Destruction upon some community, he sometimes saw the survivors gathering together, struggling to give aid to their comrades. As Za'afiel, he had not understood how the myriad tragedies he had inflicted upon them could bring out the best of these Humans. Now, Adam Kadmon understood.

The stairs were impassible for mortal flesh, so Adam simply threw survivors over the railing, and into the pool. One after another, he smashed his way into a ruined apartment, located any survivors, and bodily hurled them clear into the relative safety of the water. As he progressed around the remaining complex, he saw neighbor helping neighbor. People who often made little acknowledgment of each other now risked their own lives to save each other. Neighbors who, in fact, often spoke ill of one another, who spread gossip and rumor and false accusation, now worked frantically to pull bad swimmers and the old and the young from the water. They sheltered and comforted one another as the strongest among them helped the weakest out and away from the pool, to the street and to Holly.

The third floor produced only a single survivor, the rest having died from shrapnel, explosions, or the flames and smoke. Emergency responders had arrived at some point, and were already battling the fire.

Some of them were giving aid to the residents, and more than a few were shouting at Adam to get clear. Figures wrapped in rubber, metal, and plastic joined in the warrior's efforts at rescue. The handful of people he had missed were retrieved by the newcomers as they brought proper tools to the job: axes and crowbars and ropes and breathing masks. Even encumbered, they moved nearly as fast as Adam. They kept shouting at him to make way, to let them do their jobs. Finally, the warrior relented.

He did not retreat as they demanded, though. Instead, he grimly gathered the white leather coat around his mortal body and charged into the flaming wreckage of his and Holly's apartment. Shouts were as nothing to him. The fire and smoke were as nothing. The pain was as nothing. He had one more vital thing to save, if he could.

Eventually, Adam stumbled out of the burning wreckage of the apartment complex. Holly and Peter ran forward to grab him before the warrior could collapse, struggling against his weight to get their friend to the Beast. They leaned Adam against the motorcycle, who silently leant his own weight as a steady support for his gasping rider.

"What the hell took you so long?" Holly demanded, snatching clean water from a nearby medic to offer to her partner. "You got everyone out forever ago!"

Adam looked up at her. "I had to get something," he said through fits of coughing. He pulled open the folds of his coat and handed over to her the polished wood case that held her small harp.

Holly took the case, the only item she now owned, with wide, tear-filled eyes. She took the heavy case in her small hands with gentleness only love could allow, caressing the soot-stained wood. "You asshole!" she thundered. "You risked your life, just for this!?!"

"You're welcome," Adam coughed.

Holly continued berating him, even as she held her harp, a gift from her aunt and uncle which was more precious to her than nearly anything, to her heart. She yelled at her partner, as they stood, watching their home burn.

"Could this have been an accident?" Isandro asked.

Adam just gave him a flat look, holding the oxygen mask to his mouth and nose. The medic named Jason, the same young man who had treated him so many times before, was finishing with him. The damage had been superficial, with minor burns to Adam's head and hands, and a great deal of smoke inhalation. Most of the medic's work had been simply to give the warrior fresh, nourishing air, and to clean his head and hands.

"Who?" the good cop asked, his voice low.

"Orobas," Holly answered. She and Peter were sitting in the ambulance, opposite Adam and the medic. With the arrival of Jason the medic, Holly had stripped her own white leather coat and taken Adam's as well, hanging them from the rear doors. Even from a safe distance, the heat from the burning apartments was enough that both coats were already nearly dry.

"Who the hell is Orobas?" Isandro demanded from the back of the truck.

"Don't worry about it," Adam insisted through the cool flow of air into his lungs. "Above your pay grade."

"He can help," Holly said, not for the first time. "Or the Twins."

Adam stared hard at her and nodded at her, then jabbed a thumb at the still-burning apartment complex. Although her own coat, though lacking the mystical protection of Adam's, was still relatively undamaged, her sweater and skirt were clearly ruined. Soot stained her luminous face, and her long, dark hair hung in heavy strands.

"So what do we do?" she asked softly.

"Same plan," Adam insisted. "We run."

"Running doesn't solve a problem," Isandro pointed out.

"We need some distance," the warrior replied. "Things are too hot. Too many people are getting hurt or being put in danger. If we're gone, things'll settle down here." Distant thunder, as though mocking him, echoed through the dark sky.

"Welcome to my life," Peter said sadly, his eyes to the dim skyline. More rumbling came, from several directions. The Fallen Cherub had been the least damaged by the explosion and subsequent fire. Protected as he had been by both Adam and Holly, the apparent boy had only gotten wet, and that minor inconvenience had long since fixed itself.

Adam put a hand on the boy's knee. "We'll fix this, little brother," he promised.

"Not as long as Lilith wants this Piece," the Fallen Cherub sadly replied. "Not as long as people remain enthralled to her."

Adam leaned back, breathing deeply. There was little to say to that, since the Fallen Cherub was right. "One step at a time," the warrior half-mused. "We get clear first." He straightened and handed Jason the medic back the oxygen mask.

"So, who had 'burnt' in the pool?" Isandro asked Jason the medic.

The young man shook his head. "Life-threatening injuries only," the lifesaver casually replied before leveling a glance at Isandro. "And you know damn well who had burnt alive."

"Oh, c'mon!" the good cop insisted. "That fire was obviously life-threatening!"

"You bet on me to get burnt to death?" Adam demanded of Isandro.

The good cop shrugged.

Jason the medic shook his head. "Minor burns only, anyway. The smoke inhalation was the worst of it, and even that wasn't too bad."

"Fuck!"

"If comedy night at the burn ward is over," Adam grumbled, rubbing his head. His long, disheveled hair had apparently caught fire a few times. It was uneven now, charred in places nearly to the scalp.

There was a chorus of electronic chimes. Hands reached for devices, and illuminated screens lit up, trying to compete with the hateful glow of the burning apartment complex. "Shit," Isandro breathed.

"What now?" Adam grumbled.

"Bombs," the good cop replied, his voice empty. "All over the city." He glanced at the burning apartments. "This was just the first."

"It's us," Holly whispered, her eyes locked on her own tiny screen, its ghostly light making her already pale face seemingly even more ethereal. She looked up at Adam. "It's all against us."

"Where?" Adam asked, his chest growing cold.

"The office," his partner replied. "The entire building… it's gone." Her tiny finger danced along the glowing screen. "The Waystation, too."

"My bar," Adam growled. "Son of a bitch torched my bar."

"It's not just you guys," Isandro grimaced, also scanning the news. "There's others. The Fort Burleson museum. That shelter, *La Cocnia de Abuela.* Some house over on the south end of town."

"Kiliahoté's place," the warrior guessed. He looked to Holly and Peter. "He's targeting the Tricksters, too." Adam's eyes widened then. "Candace!"

"She's ok," Holly said, tapping on her phone. "She's with the Twins. They're at the ranch. That private security company the Twins hired has already mobilized…" She was silent, then. Her mouth parted and her breath heavy.

"What is it?" Adam demanded.

She looked up at him. "The *Daily Crier*," she replied. "The Twins' office building. It was targeted, too. It's on fire."

"He's eliminating anywhere, anyone, I might go to. He's removing possible sanctuaries."

Isandro shook his head, waving his arm for one of his people. "I'm telling you, it's not just you against you guys," he insisted. "The library's been hit, along with some empty warehouse. It's city-wide." One of his cops came over and Isandro spoke quietly with the uniformed woman.

Adam leaned in to Holly and Peter. "This will keep going as long as we're here," he told them. "Orobas won't care about any collateral damage, any lost lives. We've got to move this fight out of town."

Isandro returned. "The entire force is being mobilized," he told them. "Orders are coming down for all kinds of movement."

"What about you?" Holly asked.

"My people have been told to wait here, to secure this area," the good cop replied. He looked to the fire. "Not really sure why. Any investigation will be by the Fire Marshal, not cops."

"You've being sidelined," Adam grunted. "Orobas wants you out of the way."

A commotion drew Isandro's attention away from the ambulance. Shouts and screams were quickly followed by gunfire. The good cop drew his weapon from inside his coat and swore. "Stay here!" he barked.

"NO!" Holly screamed, grabbing their friend by the arm. He looked to her, but the young woman's dark eyes turned to Adam. "Him?" she asked in a tiny voice.

Adam only nodded and grimly stood. "Keep that pool active," he grunted to Jason the medic, pulling on his long, white leather coat.

"I've got a hundred bucks on you surviving the night," the young man replied.

Adam hopped down from the back of the ambulance. "Not a good bet," he muttered darkly. Seeing Holly and Peter moving to follow, the warrior held up a hand. "No," he commanded, his voice like granite. "I'll pull him away. He doesn't care about you or Peter. Get to the Twins."

"No!" Holly snapped, pulling her own coat over her still soaked, torn, and soot-stained skirt and sweater "No more of this lone gunslinger bullshit! We stick together!" she insisted, stepping in front of Adam.

Screams drew their attention back to the barricade. Three cops were staggering away, cradling bloody stumps that used to be hands. More gunfire shattered the deepening night. Adam put a hand on Holly's shoulder. "You promised to help the boy, remember?" he asked as gently as his harsh voice allowed. "He's the priority."

"So are you!" she countered insistently, almost desperately.

Adam shook his head. A cop was hurled over one of the patrol cars, tumbling end over end in a bloody mess that finally hit the ground with a wet thump. "Pull your people back," the warrior told Isandro. "Try to clear the area."

The good cop nodded and began barking orders into his small radio.

Adam took a step around Holly, but she grabbed his arm. "No!" she said again.

"Holly," the warrior almost whispered. "You heard how important Peter is, what he's carrying. You have to keep him safe. That's our mission, our responsibility." He glanced at Isandro. "Help her," he asked. "Get her to the Twins."

Isandro nodded and led Holly and Peter back.

Emergency vehicles began pulling back, away from the street in front of the still-burning apartment complex. Cops abandoned their hopeless assault on the Fallen Angel of Destruction, instead following Isandro's commands to clear away innocent bystanders. Behind them, the ambulance also rolled back. Within moments, a great, empty ring of steel and rubble had opened around Adam.

The warrior stood, waiting. He did not have long to wait.

Chezef also emerged from the opening ring of ruin. His dark coat was shiny in the bloody, reflected light of the fire. His unkept hair dripped with the gore of those who had tried to block him, to keep him from his vengeance. His face was scared, but fixed, his gaze upon Adam. His long blades were already in his hands. Despite the recent violence, they were clean and pure, as clean and pure as only unpolluted hate could make a thing. Blood and violence could not stick to those weapons, Adam knew.

"The violence never stuck to mine either," he called out to his once-brother.

Chezef spared a glance down at his weapons. They gleamed in the cold, hard night.

"I always wondered how they stayed so clean," Adam continued. "Despite everything we did."

"They're pure," Chezef replied. "Uriel always told us to be like them."

"'Let duty slip clean from you, even as it slips clean from your blades.'"

"I always hated his speeches," the Fallen Angel of Destruction admitted.

"He gave enough of them," Adam agreed.

"He tried another one on me, when I refused the order to kill the rebels."

"Didn't work?"

Chezef shook his head, just slightly, his eyes locked upon his brother. "Did you get a speech, before you Fell?"

Adam nodded. "Duty, duty, duty. That about summed it up."

"It's all he knew. All he cared about. He sure as Hell didn't care about us."

"He did," Adam argued, "in his way."

"Yeah," Chezef snorted. "He cared so much he sent you to purge me." The Fallen's already hard eyes darkened further, disappearing into twin voids of unforgiving wrath. "And you did. You tried."

"Duty," Adam echoed again. "Uriel told me… it doesn't matter." The warrior shook his head. "We were ordered to fight, and you refused."

"I refused to kill our brothers and sisters!" Chezef roared. "I didn't want Celestial blood on these blades! More death! More blood! More of it all! I'd had enough!"

"And now?" Adam asked, almost gently.

Chezef stared at his once-brother. "I'm over it. Centuries alone will do that. Centuries of being hunted by your own will do that. Centuries of waiting will do that." The Fallen squared himself, settling into the same stance Adam himself had used so many times before. The shoulders, the arms, the legs, the unwavering stance all spoke of the inevitability of what must happen.

"All these centuries," a new voice said, "and you haven't changed a bit."

Both of the Fallen Angels of Destruction glanced to the side. The flames of the ruined apartment complex gathered together and opened, letting pass a new arrival.

"Simkiel," Chezef sneered.

The Watcher smiled. "Hello, old friend."

"We're not friends," the Fallen growled.

"True, we were never friends." Simkiel took off the silk coat he was wearing and folded it over one arm. He was untouched by the flames, the smoke, or the despair of the Humans who were, even at that moment, letting go of their mortality and traveling towards what awaited them. The Angel continued approaching Chezef, casually rolling up the long sleeves of his designer shirt, heedless of Winter's icy grip. "I think we were never friends because, in truth, we all just pitied you too much."

Chezef said nothing; he just stared daggers at the Watcher and remained at the ready.

Adam saw what was unfolding and realized, with a start, Simkiel's purpose. The warrior's thoughts went back to the summer, when a scene much like this one had occurred, when Simkiel had said many of these same words, and why he had done it.

"Centuries here on Earth," Simkiel mused. "Living alone, always on the move." He looked at Chezef through his long, blonde eyelashes, lashes that matched his perfectly-coifed hair. "Never learning a Human's name or anything about them. And, of course, all those you sent hurtling into the Pit. Anyone with the misfortune to cross your path." Simkiel titled his head slightly. "You never showed any remorse for abandoning us, for taking your vengeance out on other Fallen. But we know the truth." The Angel smiled, spreading his arms. "Even if you weren't an Angel of Destruction, you were still a destructive creature.

"You couldn't stop your violent nature," Simkiel goaded without a glance towards Adam. The warrior backed slowly away, careful not to draw his vengeful brother's attention away from the posturing Watcher. "You just had to lash out at someone, anyone, within your reach. Did you know that you were being steered, Chezef?" Simkiel put a hand to his heart. "Sometimes it was me or one of the other Watchers, but most often it was one of the Tricksters. Whenever there was a problem, something or someone protected by Free Will, you were steered towards it. For all your talk about turning away from the Chorus, about being a free agent, you've still spent all these centuries as a tool of violence." The Angel glanced around the desolate neighborhood. "And now, here you are. Again."

Adam kept backing slowly away. Over his shoulder he saw Holly helping Peter onto the Beast.

"What do you want, Simkiel?" the warrior heard Chezef demand.

"I want to put you out of your misery," the Angel replied. "I want all your self-imposed suffering to end. I want all this destruction you cause to be over."

Adam reached the Beast. He took the wooden case from Holly that held her beloved harp. Handing it to Isandro, the warrior only said, "We'll be back for it, if we can," and mounted.

The good cop nodded, accepting the wooden case.

Behind Adam, Holly took the passenger seat, settling Peter between them. Because his little brother was imprisoned in such a small body, and Holly herself was so naturally tiny, the two of them fit without much need for the Beast to extend the rear seat. "Go!" Holly urgently whispered.

Adam hit the Beast's clutch and spurred the bike into the night. The last he heard from behind was Chezef's realization, and the roar of "NO!"

13

"So, where to?" Holly's voice came as a whisper in Adam's ear. After the battle with the *Drest-Vidar*, their old helmets had been ruined. Adam had been content without, hoping that Holly's attention would be so fixated on finding the mysterious boy-caller that she would not give thought, but this was, in retrospect, foolish. The girl's labyrinthine mind was able to focus on many annoyances, grievances, and domineering projects all at the same time. She had acquired replacements while still working to find Peter.

"We need some distance" Adam declared, encouraging more speed from the bike. He did not bother shouting. Among the other additions to these new helmets was some arcane communications system. Holly had proudly shown Adam during her grand unveiling of the uncomfortable head-gear, nearly all of which the warrior had either ignored or not understood. "He'll keep following," Adam said into the helmet, knowing his words would be transmitted to Holly's. "But we can stay ahead long enough to mask our trail." The warrior glanced over his shoulder at the rapidly-retreating hellish glow that had once been their home. The built-in visor somehow darkened in bright light; but in the Winer darkness pressing in around them, it was clear. "Besides, Orobas is after Peter. He'll try something again."

"We don't have to do this alone," Holly's voice pointed out through the small speaker close to Adam's ear.

"Yeah," Adam argued, "we do. This is my job now."

"Ours," Holly insisted, tightening her arms around both Peter and Adam.

Adam directed the Beast towards the highway that ran east and west through the heart of Disanté. It was a risk to head for such a high-profile road, the warrior knew, but they needed speed more than anything else.

"Oh shit," Holly's voice came through the helmet.

"What?" the warrior asked, glancing around at the darkened streets blurring past them.

"News is coming out," she replied. "We're being blamed for the bombs!"

"I've told you not to play with your phone when we're riding!" Adam grumbled.

"It comes through my visor, grandpa," Holly sighed in exasperation. "Hang on, the Twins are calling." She muttered whatever incantation activated her helmet and there was a soft click from the tiny speaker.

"-being blamed for everything," Harun's voice came through mid-sentence. "Orobas is planting stories with every media outlet he can."

"Including yours?" Adam growled, angry at the new problem.

"Of course not, big brother," Harun answered in near-exasperation. Adam had meant his words to only be for himself, lost in the Beast's roar. Unfortunately, as often happened, the warrior forgot about the infernal technology Holly had implanted in his helmet.

"How bad is it?" Holly's voice asked.

"Only local for right now," Harun answered. Marun's voice came from the background, though too far away to make out. "A couple of regional outlets are picking it up, but only as a minor story."

"What does that mean for us?" Holly asked.

"Local law enforcement will be out in force," the Twins replied. "Your faces are being circulated. They're saying you kidnapped a young boy."

"Fuck," Adam growled.

"It's only a matter of time before Orobas' political contacts in Austin make this a state-wide issue," the Twins continued. "The longer you're out, the worse this will get."

"And if we move across state lines," Adam almost snarled, "it becomes a federal issue." The warrior turned the Beast away from the highway. Instead, he turned into the twisting maze of neighborhoods that ran adjacent.

"Hang on, Haymer's calling." Holly again recited one of the techno-arcanic commands into her helmet.

"What in the name of sweet baby Jesus are you two idiots doing?" The Ranger lieutenant sounded nearly as irritated as Adam.

"It wasn't us!" Holly declared. "We're being set up!"

"I know that," Haymer replied. "You'd have to be some kind of short bus moron to fall for such an obvious set up." There was a rustling of papers and some muted talk in the background. "Well, like I said," the Ranger sighed. "Look, the Disanté mayor is trying to call in State help to round you two up. So far, our beloved governor isn't biting, but it's only a matter of time. We've got to get you two into protective custody before this gets out of hand."

"He's after the boy," Adam growled. "We come in, they get the boy."

"I can get you two out of Meropis County," Haymer replied. "The Rangers'll keep you safe, I swear it. Just come in."

There was another click and Holly's voice was a soft whisper in Adam's ear. "We have to trust someone," she said in a gentle command.

Adam glanced back at her. A mistake, he realized, as her large, twin eyes of shining black sincerity ended any possible argument. "Fine," he grumbled.

Another click. "Where do we go?" Holly said to Haymer.

"I've got a team at Georgetown," the Ranger replied. "They're waiting for you. They'll get you to a safehouse on the other side of Austin. I'm a few hours out; likely I'll be there around dawn. Haul ass."

Adam grunted and steered the Beast south.

"Take 19 south," Holly commanded, pointing over Adam's shoulder to the turn.

"I know," Adam grunted, turning. Like so many of Texas' highways, this one ran through the middle of town. There were frequent traffic lights and stop signs, all of which the Beast ignored. The streets were deserted and most of the lights were extinguished. Long shadows reached out, clawing at them as they raced down the four-lane road. The small group passed one of the commercial districts, with its used car dealerships, pawn shops, beauty parlors, and fast-food chains. Everything was dark and silent.

"I know that growl," Holly noted. "What's wrong?"

"Where is everybody?" the warrior growled. "It's the weekend. It's the holidays. Why's it so quiet?"

"An alert went out," she pointed out, probably consulting her helmet. "All citizens are warned to stay indoors. Dangerous fugitives on the loose. Police are… crap."

Peter said something that Adam could not hear over the roar of the wind. "What was that?" he asked Holly.

"Orobas is planning something," she relayed. "He wants the streets clear. He'll have a trap ready."

"Yup." Adam leaned forward slightly. "Hang on," he commanded. "Our only chance is to out run whatever he's setting up." The Beast needed no encouragement, roaring even louder and racing into the night.

They approached what the soldiers of Fort Burleson called the entertainment district. Several strip clubs and bars lined both sides of the road. Bright neon encouraged the weary and the lonely and the lustful to come in an enjoy women in various states of undress. Normally, the parking lots were filled beyond capacity. Harsh music would spill out from these pits of despair, blending together into a swamp of sin. Normally, pockets of celebrants would wander from one business to the next, swaying more unsteadily as the night progressed. As late as it had become, there should have been dozens of these small groups and a great many individuals, all either seeking out more illusions of intimacy or staggering home, still alone but without money.

Instead, it was dark and quiet. There was no neon glow, painting the streets with their unnatural colors. There was no ugly blend of harsh music. There were no patrons, lustfully moving from one show to the next. There was only the night, and Winter's grip tightening around them.

They passed the clubs and the bars, continuing south. The county line lay ahead. Just beyond, outside of the nominal legal authority of Disanté government, was Nova. At the end of the line of adult entertainment was a small gap, an open field separating these more upstanding businesses from Nova. The large building, a converted barn, stood apart from its brethren. It had only a single neon sign, one of an exploding star, high atop what had once been a windmill. Nova was an all-nude establishment, something forbidden within Meropis County. Most patrons, though, came from Fort Burleson, so the owner set up his club as close to the base as possible while still outside the legal restrictions of Disanté. This made the club the unofficial county line.

Unlike the other strip clubs, Nova's sign was alight, shining like a beacon, calling to them. Once they reached Nova, they were beyond Orobas' direct authority. The Fallen Watcher would have to rely on political favors and criminal connections to pursue them, and that would take time. Adam would be able to use that time to throw off Chezef. All they needed to do was reach Nova.

The Beast came to a screeching halt. The bike and his three passengers sat and stared for a moment, before Adam said, "Damn."

Just ahead of Nova and the county line, arrayed across the entire road, was a line of police vehicles. Their flashing lights blended together with the neon glow of the windmill behind them, combining into a golden glow that teased at Adam and his friends, taunting them with sanctuary that was utterly out of reach.

"HANG ON!" Adam roared, joined by the Beast.

They leapt into the wide field marking the boundary of Meropis County. The ground was wildly uneven, with the Beast repeatedly dipping into an unseen depression only to leap into the air. Together, bike and rider tried to guide their course, to move them away from the roadblock but still towards the relative safety of the next county, despite the rugged terrain.

Headlights erupted in front of them. A team of six vehicles appeared between them and the county line, charging towards the Beast and his passengers. They were police vehicles, perhaps, painted in the dark blue and bearing the signs and sigils of Disanté's peace keepers. They were low things, open-top single-seaters with four large wheels and powerful engines. These utility bikes handled the rough terrain with much greater agility then could the two-wheeled Beast.

"Damn!" Adam growled and used the next incline to shift their course away from the new arrivals. The quads surrounded them in seconds. One of the riders drew close and aimed something at Adam. The warrior jerked the Beast towards that cop, forcing the rider to swerve away. There was a snap and a sparking hiss as something impacted against the Beast's gas tank. "They want us alive," Adam grumbled as the stun prongs fell away.

Another rider approached from the opposite side, already taking aim with his stun gun. The crack of Holly's gun snapped from behind Adam. Despite the extreme maneuvering, despite the almost constant up and down, low jumps and hard landings, somehow she was pinpoint in her aim. Three quick shots struck the quad to their side and its rider lost control. The small vehicle hit an embankment and spun, flipping into the darkness.

"I can't reload in all this!" Holly declared, using measured shots to keep the riders at bay.

Adam grunted and made another sudden turn, aiming once more for the county line. Two quads darted forward, their superior acceleration and maneuverability better able to handle the rough terrain. The riders shot ahead and turned, blocking Adam's intended path. He swore as the Beast was forced away, back into Meropis County. Even as the bike turned, the quads once again began surrounding them.

"They're driving us!" Holly yelled. "Like cowboys driving a stray back to the herd!"

"Damn," Adam growled and turned them back towards the highway. The quads pursued only until the Beast was on paved road and heading back into Disanté.

"I'm getting a text..." Holly noted. "It's from... Adam, it's from Orobas."

"Well?" the warrior asked flatly.

"It's just one word. 'Predictable.'"

Adam snarled and hit the Beast's clutch. The bike reared and roared his own frustration, to match his riders as they sped back into Orobas' domain.

"Now where?" Holly asked. Even with the aid of the communication system in their helmets, she had to shout over the combined roars of the Beast, the wind, and Adam's growing rage.

"East," he spat. "Through Parker Place to Chrisville. We'll cut south at Bolton."

Adam took them not towards the commercial distractions and better residential areas that lined the main highway, but through the back roads. There were no traffic lights here, working or not. There were no street signs. Most often, there were no paved streets at all. One dirt road gave way to another, and another. The Beast twisted from one unmarked path to another, his amber gaze the only illumination for miles. A horrid cloud of dust gathered around them, held back only by their speed. Adam could feel Holly press herself and Peter close into his back, she no doubt trying to shield the boy from the unbreathable air.

Worse, the roads they traveled began attacking them, tossing up rocks and other debris. Adam said nothing, nor ducked into the howling wind. He kept his back rigid, an impenetrable shield behind which Holly and Peter could shelter against the dirt, the wind, the rocks, and the evil night ahead. The white leather coat shielded Adam's body from the worst of the road's attacks, though he had no doubt his body would be a patchwork of bruises. The sheer number of the missiles, though, soon won out. Warm blood soon covered Adam's unprotected hands, and the warrior cursed himself for not thinking to wear gloves.

"Not a great outfit for night riding," Holly voice came softly through the small speaker in Adam's helmet. He risked a glance back and down. The skirt she had worn was torn and filthy, little more than rags now and offering almost no protection against the wind. Worse, the need to straddle the Beast forced the skirt up high, exposing nearly all of her tiny legs to Winter's bite and the road's angry attacks. The warm winter leggings she had worn were in tatters. Strips of fabric fluttered in the wind, exposing Holly's pale flesh. Her own white leather coat could have protected her, but she had insisted on wrapping it around Peter. Blood, fresh and old, stained what remained of those leggings. Her arms, wrapped around Adam's middle, were showing similar damage. Her cheerful sweater was growing more torn and stained. Her skin pimpled against Winter's growing fury and the savage roads through which they fled. Despite all this, her tiny hands were firm, her grip unflinching, as she sheltered Peter between her tiny body and Adam's.

The Beast responded immediately when his rider turned him off the dirt roads and back towards the harsh light of civilization. "Aren't we vulnerable going this way?" Holly asked, trying to hide the relief in her voice when the ride smoothed and the road's attacks relented.

"We move faster this way," Adam lied.

Parker Place was little more than a sprawling hive of trailer parks. The poorest of Disanté's residents lived out here. These supposedly mobile homes ranged from wide encampments with gardens and amenities, to small metallic coffins, isolated amongst large rocks and choking weeds. The greed of the land's owners meant little or nothing was done to make Parker Place more habitable, more comfortable for the people condemned to living there. The place had no schools or libraries. The decaying bodies of innumerable burnt and ruined trailers spoke of the lack of emergency services. Even communications were limited in Parker Place; the residents stared with hollow eyes as Adam led his friends through that pit, clearly having not been told to shelter indoors or not caring if Death finally freed them from that monument to Humanity's indifference.

Adam gave no thought or second glace to any of the hopeless residents as they sped through Parker Place. These people were not an immediate threat, and therefore of no concern to the warrior. Instead, he guided the Beast through the twisting maze of small roads towards the lone shining point in that shunned region.

The boundary to the Superstore was sudden and obvious. Their bone-jarring passage through Parker Place's unkept roads instantly gave way to the pavement of modern capitalism. Tall light posts shone down on the empty lot. The giant store itself, a temple for cheap and cheaply-made goods, was obviously open and inviting.

The Beast raced through the empty parking lot and towards the nearby onramp for the highway. Once free of the dirt roads of Parker Place, the bike accelerated, obviously relieved to have left the uneven path behind in favor of the smooth streets ahead. They shot up the onramp, becoming briefly airborne as the pavement leveled out onto the highway and left the access ramps behind.

"Are we clear?" Holly asked.

In response, Adam again yanked at the Beast, pulling the bike to a stop. They all sat and stared ahead. Another line of flashing police vehicles sat upon the highway, just before the next access ramps. "Damn," Adam grunted.

"Orobas texted again," Holly said numbly.

"Yeah, I can guess," Adam almost snarled.

"Is he tracking our phones?" she asked.

"He doesn't have to," Peter replied. "He would have planned this well in advance." The Fallen Cherub leaned over to look up at Adam. "We're doing exactly what he wants."

"I know!" Adam snapped. The warrior looked around, trying to think.

"You're not going to out-plan him," Peter said gently. "You can't out-think him. He wants you to run, so you run into his trap."

A light shown down on them from above. They looked up and saw a police helicopter hovering far overhead, it's spotlight marking them.

"Why aren't they shooting or chasing us or something?" Holly asked.

"They want me alive," Peter told her. "If I die, the Piece I carry will be lost to them. As long as we stay in Meropis County, they'll keep back."

"They're the dogs," Adam countered, looking around. "They're guiding the hunter."

"Chezef?" Holly asked.

"He'll just follow them. He knows they'll be near us. He kills me; they get Peter."

"So, what do we do?"

Adam straightened and reoriented the Beast. "West," he declared. "Cappa Caves, then south. We'll get through this."

The warrior ended any more debate by gunning the Beast's engine. He did not bother with side streets or evasion. Orobas would be ready for that, he knew. Instead, he remained on the straight lanes of the highway, unleashing the Beast to build up incredible speed as they shot through the middle of Disanté.

"I'm pretty sure that helicopter is still back there," Holly said nervously.

"It's there," Adam grunted, encouraging even more speed out of the Beast.

"How do we lose them?" she asked. "It can just fly over us and keep us in sight."

A though occurred to Adam. He looked to the south as they neared the far edge of Disanté, to the large open field and the landing strips of the new regional airport. "Keep hold of him!" the warrior barked.

He felt Holly grip his belt from behind and push herself, and thus Peter, as tightly as possible into his back. Adam adjusted the Beast's course; he did not take them to another access ramp, though, but instead made for one of the open areas on the support hills. The highway was elevated; it loomed over the city streets. Although much of this was supported with concrete pillars, there were also artificial hills from time to time. On these, the walls that surrounded the highway vanished, allowing for an open view of the surrounding area. Adam pointed the Beast towards one of these. He stood, gripping the bike with his bent knees and leaned forward of the handlebars.

"HOLY SHIT!" Holly exclaimed as they launched off of the elevated highway and into the sky.

The Beast gave a triumphant roar as he leapt free of the ground.

"Hold still for fuck's sake!" Adam barked, his eyes locked on the landing point. He eased the Beast's front end forward, towards the steep slope of the artificial hill. He eased the throttle up in the instant before they touched down.

"IHATETHISWHATISWRONGWITHYOUASSHOLENEVERD OTHATAGAINIDIOTTHERESAKIDWITHUSSTUPIDSONOFABI TCH-"

Adam tuned out Holly's rant as he and the Beast steadied and sped down the artificial hill, gaining even more speed.

"What even was the point of that you idiot moron asshole!?!" Even through her rage, Holly maintained her iron grip on Adam, crushing both herself and Peter against his immovable torso. Some abstract part of the warrior's mind, that part that not only remained calm, but grew more serene with increasing crisis, noticed something.

"Did you know your accent gets thicker when you're angry?" Adam pointed out.

"You damned brain-dead, numbnuts, fopdoodle!" she raged, emphasizing a few syllables with strikes to his back and head. "What the hell you mean, talkin' that trash!?!"

"Normally, you don't really have an accent," he pointed out with a slight shrug.

Holly's venomous response continued all the way to their destination.

"Well," she snapped when the Beast came to a stop. "What in high hell are we doin' here?"

In response, Adam only pointed at the entrance sign of Disanté Regional Airport as they sped past. He guided them through the parking lot and towards an access gate.

"You're just about as sharp as mashed potatoes!" Holly pointed out. "It's closed and locked!"

In response, Adam reared the Beast up onto his back wheel just before they reached the chain linked fence. The Bike, sensing his rider's intent, punched through the weak metal with his forward wheel and shot through onto the airstrip.

"I. Hate. You." Holly said with the absolute calmness females only ever seemed to achieve with males.

The Beast carried them across the various smaller airstrips and the large main one, towards a series of hangers on the far side of the field. The hangers were unlit, but still illuminated by the airport's lights and the overhead Moon. Adam led them inside the main doors, pulling to a stop beside the small, single-propeller plan inside.

"We can rest a moment," he declared, deploying the Beast's kickstand.

Holly detached herself from Adam and dismounted. She carefully pulled free her helmet and turned to face her partner. She raised a hand, pointing an accusatory finger at him, her entire tiny body shaking with the need to savage him.

Adam only looked at her with a flat, emotionless expression.

Holly turned and walked away, muttering to herself.

"Do you have a plan?" Peter asked calmly.

Adam helped the Fallen Cherub dismount and then stretched his legs. "This'll buy us a little time. The cops won't be able to follow right away. The airspace is restricted, so that copter will have to stay away. This airfield is only borrowed by Disanté. It's technically Federal land. Orobas will need a little time to get access."

"Then what?" Holly snapped.

"And then we think of something," Adam replied. "We needed to do something unexpected, so…" he gestured around the hanger.

"Is this really all that unexpected?" Peter asked.

"What do you mean?"

"Lot's wife," the apparent boy replied. "You were only supposed to kill her, but you decided to do something spectacular instead. Or when you made King Jehoram's bowels fall out, when he was only supposed to die of a fever. Or how about Absalom? You hanged him with his own hair."

The Fallen Cherub began ticking examples off his small fingers. "You killed Herod Agrippa by having him get eaten alive by worms. You dropped a tortoise on Aeschylus' head. You drowned Jing of Jin in a toilet. You lured Susima of Ind into a fiery pit. You convinced the Parthians to pour molten gold town Crassus' throat. You dragged Basil I for 16 miles. There's that business with Edgar Allen Poe in Baltimore. And I think the less said about your visit with the Donner Party, the better."

"A tortoise?" Holly asked in a tiny voice. "A cute little turtle?"

"It wasn't a…" Adam shook off her selective empathy and rounded on Peter. "What's the point?" he demanded. He added, under his breath, "damn thing weighed almost eight stone."

"Orobas will be ready for this," Peter insisted. "He was your Watcher for a long time. He even kept track of your activities after the Rebellion. He knows how you think. You always make the big displays, these dramatic statements. Subtlety has never been one of your virtues, any more than teamwork. You have to do what he wouldn't expect."

"How the Hell am I supposed to do that!?!" the warrior demanded. "How am I supposed to think of something I wouldn't think of?"

"By asking for help," Holly said firmly. She stepped towards him, tucking her helmet under her arm. "Everything you do, every problem, every crisis, your first instinct is to go it alone. When we fought the *Drest-Vidar*, your first instinct was to fight them alone. When..." her voice caught a moment. "When the cult... when my parents..." She took a deep, steadying breath. "You didn't ask for help. Isandro told me he offered to help you fight them, to come and get me. But you wanted to do it alone."

"You've always fought alone, Adam," Peter added, standing beside Holly. "The other Angels of Destruction worked together, but you always stood alone."

Holly moved closer and put a hand on Adam's arm. "But you're not alone. You don't have to do this alone. You've got me. You've got the Twins. You've got Isandro and Haymer. We're your friends. Let us help you."

"Orobas is counting on you to stand alone," Peter said then. "He's counting on you to do what you always do: fight alone."

Adam said nothing, trying but failing to avoid the bottomless pools that were Holly's wide, dark eyes. "People will get hurt..." he tried to say.

"That's our choice," Holly insisted. "We choose who to stand with. We chose to fight."

Peter walked to the edge of the hanger and looked out. In the distance, at the edge of the airport, flashing police lights were approaching. "Orobas has the local government," the Fallen Cherub pointed out. "He has politicians and police. He even called in Chezef." The boy turned. "But you're still trying to do this alone."

"Run," Holly said, repeating one of Adam's favorite points. "Fight. Deal. Hide. Those are the choices, right? But you don't have to run, fight, deal, or hide alone." She squeezed his arm. "You promised to protect Peter, just like you promised to protect me." She gestured to the horizon and all their approaching enemies. "Is this protecting us?"

Adam took a deep breath and sighed, closing his hard eyes. "No," he admitted.

"So how to you protect us?"

"Chezef is the immediate threat," the warrior considered. "But Orobas is the real problem."

"So how do we beat him?" Holly asked.

"He uses the shadows," Peter said. "He advises, he manipulates, but always from behind the ones in power. From safety. But he's arrogant. He thinks he's smarter than everyone and loves to show off."

"So we tempt him into the light," Adam mused, an idea forming. "We get him to show himself." He looked to Holly, tapping a finger on her helmet. "How far do these reach? The communication?"

She shrugged. "I never tested, but about 500 yards, I think."

The warrior nodded. "Good enough. You and Peter take the Beast, go to the far end of the airport without all the lights. I'll signal when to pick me up." He grabbed his own helmet. "Call the Twins, tell them…" He took another deep breath. "Tell them I need help."

"What's the plan?" Holly asked, reaching for her phone.

Adam glanced at Peter. "I always do the big flashy thing, right?"

"Yes."

The warrior shrugged and glanced towards an area separated from all the hangers and surrounded with warning signs. "Well, then I'll give Orobas what he's waiting for."

By the time Adam was ready, the Twins had their own media in place. Several helicopters were circling the airport's restricted space, with cameras pointing in. As the combined eyes the Twins commanded, along with Orobas' peace officers, watched in horror, Adam ignited the airport's fuel dump. The fireball blazed into the night sky, briefly forcing away Winter's approach. From the inferno Adam had started, a single line of fire streamed out, along the ground. As though some angry god of wrath and ruin were tracing along the pavement, Adam's message to both Chezef and Orobas was spelled out in fiery letters.

GRIFFIN RESORT. ONE HOUR.

14

The Griffin Resort had been the playground of Texas' wealthy. Cattle and oil barons, iron mongers, slum lords, and tech bros had all used the sprawling campus to escape the pressure of squeezing their neighbors of every possible coin. The several pools, connected with a perfectly-controlled lazy river, had offered relief from the Texas heat. The many bars and lounges had provided every possible intoxicant. Gun ranges and horseback trails and live music had all provided what the wealthy believed to be an authentic Texas experience. The suites had been tastefully decorated, with only subtle gold inlaid in the walls and furniture. The staff had been pliant and eager, providing quick service for whatever whims their guests experienced. The private security had been protective of the resort's privacy, keeping away nosy reporters or the intrusive poor. Griffin had been an oasis for the rich and powerful.

Now, it was in the midst of what the owners and management called a renovation. Like the claws of a dying beast, construction cranes enfolded the main building. To Adam's eyes, the capitalistic monster was either trying to save itself from its grave, or drag the vacation home of the ultra-wealthy along with it. Half-finished projects were scattered across the grounds like a spoiled child's abandoned toys, ideas and ambitions that were dreamt of but then cast aside against their monetary cost. Abandoned protest signs, objecting to more of the destruction of the wetlands surrounding the river, littered the collapsing fence surrounding the dark resort. Winter had come, ending all work at Griffin.

Adam guided the Beast through the open gate without a backwards glance. Orobas' minions were still following, he knew. Although they had escaped the airport and even managed to evade detection for a short time, the aerial surveillance had discovered Adam and those he had sworn to protect long before they had reached the Twin's ranch. He had not given them time enough to surround the protected compound, though, staying only long enough to deposit Holly and Peter and brief everyone on what he needed them to do. He had remained mounted on the Beast, intending to ride immediately away, but Candace had caused a brief delay.

The Twins had given her a change of clothes after she took shelter with them. When she had appeared in the front doors of the large house, Adam had forced himself not to stare. Her long, auburn hair was still free, still spilling like an autumnal waterfall down her shoulders. She still wore jeans, but had traded her shirt and coat for a long, flowing white sweater that fell to her thighs. Though it seemed baggy, the sweater still hugged her curves, subtly drawing the eye to Candace's feminine lines. The bartender had also donned a knitted cap and scarf matching her sweater to protect from the worsening cold. As Adam briefed Holly and the Twins, the warrior had to fight to keep his eyes and attention fixed on the battle to come.

She had walked towards him as he finished telling them his plan. Walked, Adam had realized in that moment, was an imprecise word. Candace had not walked. She had seemed, just then, incapable of something as mundane as walking. The few steps leading down from the Twin's front porch were already covered in a light coating of ice, but Candace seemed unaffected. Her booted feet never lost purchase, never seemed hesitant as she had drawn closer. She did not glide, being so firmly connected to the Earth. In fact, she had not seemed to move at all, really. Instead, the world had conspired to draw her closer to Adam, to close the distance between them, until she was standing at the Beast, looking down at him.

"So," she said, the scent of her breath and her body fuzzing the edges of Adam's mind. "You're gonna fight him?"

"This has to end," Adam had said, desperately holding onto the cold indifference that had seen him though so many battles. "None of you will be safe as long as he knows I'm out here."

"I'm not arguin'," she had almost whispered, drawing Adam closer with her gentle voice. The bartender had traced a light touch along the edge of his white leather coat. "Nor objectin'," she added.

"I wish," Adam had started to say, only dimly aware of the Twins leading Holly and Peter away, despite Holly's attempts at staying and watching. The warrior had been unable to finish his thought.

Candace had nodded. "I know." She had leaned in slightly, closing only half the distance. "Bein' the woman of a mysterious stranger ain't easy." She had shrugged. "But I knew that."

Adam was unable to move, his resolve to stay cold and empty against what had lain ahead crumbling. "If there was time…"

"We only get so much" she had reminded him. "All of us only just get so much time. Means we have to take advantage, when she comes around."

"I'm sorry that I-" Cadance had put a finger on his lips.

She had shaken her head slightly. "Don't apologize for past sins," she had said. "What's done, can't be undone. Just make it right tomorrow."

The warrior had shaken his head. "I have to face my brother," he had reminded her. "I likely don't have a tomorrow."

"Then make it right today."

Adam had been unsure of what to do, how to proceed. He was a warrior, a bringer of destruction. That was all the life he had ever known, or ever cared to. Violence, slaughter, betrayal, horror, these were things he was comfortable with. Candace, however, was none of these things; she embodied something utterly alien to Adam. He had sat, unable to close the small distance separating them, and was about to grab the handlebars when the Beast took action.

The bike under him had jerked suddenly to the side, forcing Adam against Candace. His eyes widened in shock for only a second. Then he put his free arm around her waist and drew her in tightly. Candace had given a brief squeak of surprise before melting into the kiss. She wrapped her arms around the back of his neck and opened herself to him. Her breath had come faster, heavier, with greater heat. Her hands had clenched into nails, digging into his back and his unkempt hair. Her probing of him, her exploration, had grown more urgent, more demanding.

Adam had once again been unsure of what to do, and once more the Beast had acted. The bike under him jerked once more, tearing the warrior away from the bartender. His engine had ignited with a roar and he slowly pulled forward. Candace had released her grip on Adam, though she had also let her fingers linger as they withdrew. He had looked back only once as he and the Beast left behind the Twin's ranch, seeing Candace standing at the edge of the walkway where they had left her, holding up one hand to him.

"Thanks," he had said to his bike.

The Beast had grumbled an affirmative.

But that was then, and this was now, the warrior realized as they continued slowly towards the front of the Griffin Resort's main building. He had needed the short ride from the ranch to clear his unwanted soul of harmful things. Compassion was weakness. Gentleness was death. Only hard, unforgiving violence ensured survival. And yet, something in what Candace had said to him lingered. Her scent refused to fade, her touch refused to pass, her taste…

The warrior shook his head angrily, damning such soft thoughts.

The Beast arrived at the front of the resort's main building. The hole was still there, open and ready like the maw of some great beast of legend. After the incident in Autumn, the owners had decided to take the opportunity to remodel. The car that had crashed through the front doors, trying to run down Adam and Holly, had been removed. With it had gone nearly the entire front wall. Adam dismounted and removed the helmet Holly had forced upon him. His eyes took in the hollowed-out building. "You know what to do?" he asked the bike.

The Beast rumbled an affirmative.

"No matter what," the rider insisted, glancing to the roof. "If this goes sideways, get them out of here." He took a deep breath. "After," the warrior almost whispered. "Stay with them."

The Beast rumbled again and sped off.

Adam glanced back, towards the open gate and meaningless fence. Already, he could see the cops under Orobas' control forming a perimeter. Their lights were not flashing, but their presence was undeniable in the dim, pre-dawn light. They let the Beast leave; they were only focused on Adam. They obviously had no intention of coming in, and were leaving the road open for one more arrival.

On the horizon, cresting the surrounding hills, was a single point of light against the last of the long night, drawing closer.

Adam sighed and entered the vacant building, tucking his helmet under one arm. What had been the lobby was little more than a cluster of power tools, construction materials, temporary scaffolding, and protective covers, blanketing the surviving marble. The place echoed, alone and quiet. He knew the feeling of that place, having spent most of his eternal life alone. Even in the company of his fellow Angels of Destruction, even as that building was surrounded by smaller ones, Adam had always been alone. He had offered echoing sounds to try and match the celebrations of his fellows after each harrowing mission. Adam had tried to fill the emptiness inside, like the rubble and the tools and the abandoned building materials tried to fill the hollow resort. But, it had all been a lie.

Adam wandered towards the stairwell, past the inoperable elevators. They were only for show now, an empty reminder of former work. The warrior glanced at the decorated controls, the stylized buttons and doors, harkening back to an age long dead. He wondered if the other Angels of Destruction did that, now that he was gone. They had done so after the Rebellion, trying to maintain the idea of their service after half their siblings had waged a war of near-mutual extinction. Za'afiel had gone through the motions for centuries, hoping to find the old meaning, the old familiarity, before all the darkness. Some of the elevator controls and even a few of the doors, were in the midst of being replaced with new, modern technology. This was the way of things, Adam knew; old wounds needed to be healed.

The staircase was empty and silent, even more so than the ruined lobby. Light shone down from the great hole in the ceiling, where the owners were in the middle of installing new technology. Adam stood for a moment in that darkness. He was so used to it, after so many centuries. He had so constantly found himself in the midst of destruction he had caused, staring up towards the Silver City, as distant then as it was now. So many times over the many blood-drenched missions, the warrior had stared up and wondered if the ascent was at all worth the effort.

Adam shifted the helmet under his arm. Holly's helmet, really. She had chosen it. She had installed the communications system within it. She had forced it upon him. This was what his life had become. He had spent countless lifetimes wandering the darkness of the Earth, not really searching, but perhaps content in his silent isolation. Then, he had Holly forced upon him. Another glance towards the sky reconfirmed his knowledge that all his misery of the Summer and Autumn were deliberate. Holly's interference in his intentional self-destruction, the Twins' meddling in his actions, and even Candace's...

He began the climb. His thoughts continued to maddeningly remain with Candace even as he took one heavy step after the next up, out of that quiet, crowded isolation. The way her blue eyes sparkled in the Texas sun, the gleam of a sunset on her auburn hair, the droplets of Summer sweat that would trace down the front of her t-shirt. All of these lay before him, ahead on the next step, the next landing, as though taunting him in his climb. Her scent blanketed his mind, insulating it against the hard emptiness the warrior was trying to summon. He reached in and tried to force down Candace's warmth from his heart, to safely lock away the music of her laugh. This was how he had survived the Rebellion, how he had achieved so many vile missions for the Chorus, how he had inflicted so much horror over the countless centuries: he had pushed it all down into his personal Pit. There, the feelings could not harm him, could not threaten him. He was safe from such poisons as compassion, empathy, and… and that one emotion, most of all, he did not dare name.

But the feel of Candace's lips lingered, and the darkness beneath him continued to retreat.

Adam made his way up the staircase. He stepped over piles of rubble, of half-finished repairs and improvements. He moved past all the possible missteps and the potential to fall. He climbed up from the darkness. His eyes went up once more, to the hole in the roof and the silvery clouds, blushing against the coming dawn. The staircase through which he moved was open to the Winter sky. He saw the glittering heavens above, through the retreating canopy that had tried so hard, for so long, to cover his world. He climbed on, towards those lights, away from the inky pit through which he had entered.

The stairs ended in a landing that had only one wall and no door. Adam simply stepped out, onto the flat roof. Still, after the several floors, he could not find his warrior's cold resolve. He was still calm, though. He still had the finality of purpose, but it was unfamiliar. Always before, he had pushed down all the soft, gentle things that would make him flinch away from his duties. Always before, he had found comfort in the unfeeling void that banished such insidious, toxic things. Always before, his preparation for Destruction had been to free himself from thought, from feeling, from everything that was weak and dirty.

But now, the warrior's mind and his soul were full. He was calm, but he was also warmed from within. He did not feel Winter's oppressive touch on his exposed skin. His eyes did not linger on the dark hole from which he had emerged. Instead, his weary sight turned to the horizon.

The sky was aflame.

Rosy Dawn was at last arriving. The clouds were still heavy in the sky, but they were no longer the oppressive grey of imminent hard weather, of threats and oppression and miserable isolation. Instead, shades of red and blue, a bubblegum canvas of joy was forcing away the stubborn darkness. Beyond that, at the very edge of the world, an auburn glow was rising. Already, it hinted at a warm day to come. Already, it brushed gentle fingers across Adam's soul, tender, nourishing, and accepting of everything he was.

And, for the first time in months, for the first time since Adam Kadmon had Fallen and found himself in this rancid pit of a city, he accepted that warmth. He set down the helmet that had been a gift from his tiny friend and moved towards the edge of the broken, flawed roof. He felt the inconstant world beneath him, but he paid it little mind. He looked ahead, past the greedy work of the wealthy and the powerful and the corrupt, past the scars of modernization and industrialization, and past the hopeless misery that had already begun to wither against new hope. Adam looked to the blushing sky and the persistently-cheerful clouds and, for perhaps the first time in an eternal age, a smile drifted upon hard lips.

"One last sunrise, Za'afiel?"

The warrior did not bother turning. Orobas was not a fighter. He never made physical attacks, trusting instead such things he felt beneath him to those he manipulated. "My name is Adam," he said, putting his hands in his pockets.

"Adam Kadmon is a fiction," Orobas argued. "Something you've wrapped around your true self. It's no more what you are than that coat you stole from… what was his name?"

"Jean-Pierre Casimir," Adam replied.

"I've never understood that fascination you have with remembering their names."

The warrior turned, facing Orobas. The Fallen Watcher was dressed in a suit and tie, with a heavy winter coat to protect him from the world. One hand was casually in his pocket, the other gloved hand was holding a small pistol, pointed at Adam.

"I always remember the names," he said.

"The names of all your victims," Orobas said in derision, "forever carved into your very being in the First Language." The Fallen shook his head. "Pathetic."

"You wouldn't understand."

"More accurately, I don't care." He glanced over the side of the roof. "You're just about out of time. Chezef has arrived. You'll be dead in a few minutes." The Fallen shifted a bit, using his free hand to better close his coat against the cold. "Look, I've already had to spend more time than I care to on all this. I know full well that you've handed the boy over to the Twins. I don't have enough assets to take him back by force. I'm tired of doing things the hard way, anyway. Three damn times I've had to kidnap that little brat, and three damn times someone has taken him from me. I'll offer you just one deal. Chezef is going to kill you. I've gone to a lot of trouble to make sure you two have your reunion. I'll be cleaning up tonight's mess for months. Starting a near-riot, all the bombs, organizing the entire police force to hunt one man, closing off the city, shutting down everything for an entire night." The Fallen shook his head and took a deep, calming breath. "Messy and annoying.

"There's no possible way to call him off. And I've invested too much in this project for any more delays. After your brother is finished with you, I'll call in enough of the politicians I control to storm that ranch. I'll get the governor to send in his National Guard if I have to. I'll have the Twins and those Human girls you're so fond of framed for all the things I've done. The bombs earlier tonight, the riot at the Tree Lighting, all the killings. Hell, I'll have them blamed for all the things the *Imā* Cult and the *Drest-Vidar* did. This is a state that still executes people, don't forget. But if you call them, tell them to give me the boy, my business with them is done.

"If you tell them to give me the boy, then your women can survive, I'll allow you that. You die, I get the boy, and I'll leave them alone. Otherwise, I'll destroy their lives, make them suffer as only I know how to arrange, and eventually, I'll kill them. Another girl you promised to protect will die screaming. The Twins, your darling little sisters, will be hurled into the Pit."

Heavy bootsteps came from the same dark stairwell from which Adam had emerged. Orobas meaningfully motioned towards the sound. "Do the right thing, one last time. Call your women and give me the boy. Save the innocents once more, like you always do." He smirked. "Or rather, like you always tried to do. One last good deed, Za'afiel."

The warrior did not glance towards the approaching bootsteps. Instead, he calmly faced Orobas and said, "My name is Adam."

"Fine," the Fallen Watcher sighed in exasperation. "Well, you can't say I didn't try to be nice, this once." He glanced aside as Chezef emerged from the dark stairwell. "Too late, now."

Adam stepped back, giving his vengeful brother ample space to emerge. Chezef was still wearing the long black coat from earlier that night, and his blades were already in his hands. His brother looked almost as tired, almost as beaten, as Adam. His face was covered in dried blood and fresh wounds. His dark coat was torn in several places, its color blending with both old nad new blood. His uncovered hands were pitted with signs of the violent night. Chezef walked slowly, deliberately, his gait uneven but unflinching. The Fallen Angel of Destruction limped up, onto the roof and looked directly at Adam though one blackened eye, and the other shot with blood. He ignored Orobas, instead limping to the center of the rooftop, facing his brother and the imminent sunrise.

"Brother," Adam said.

"Brother," Chezef replied.

The two warriors, both broken and bloody, stared at each other, saying nothing, unmoving. Finally, Orobas sighed again in exasperation and put away his pistol. "Well, I can see there's no getting a word in with you two," he said casually and began walking towards the stairwell. "I'll leave you to this." The Fallen Watcher glanced hatefully at Adam. "You'll excuse me, of course. I have a ranch to assault, a boy to kidnap, and women to frame.

"One last thing," Adam said.

Orobas threw a smirk over his shoulder. "And what's that?"

Adam withdrew the phone Holly had given him weeks ago from the side pocket of his white leather coat. He raised the small device to his face and said, "Did you get all that?"

Holly's voice came through the speaker, clear and loud in the way she had shown him to arrange. "We got it," she confirmed. "The helmet captured everything."

Orobas glanced down at the helmet, at Holly's gift, where Adam had placed it near the stairs upon his arrival. The Fallen snarled and kicked away the hard thing with its imbedded technology.

"The Twins are uploading everything to all their media sources," Holly's voice continued. Below, sirens and yelling filled the air. Orobas ran to the parapet wall and looked down, his face wide in realized horror. Adam did not have to look. He knew what was happening.

Below, Isandro and his team, along with those cops who could be trusted, were surrounding those who had sold themselves to Orobas. Supplemented with Haymer's Rangers, the white hats were calling for surrender. Outnumbered, and with their employer's crimes suddenly exposed, there would be little resistance. Orobas' army, his corrupt cops, would not fight back, would submit and try to explain away their actions as having just followed orders.

"You think this achieves anything?" Orobas demanded, his eyes wide, but a sneer of furious contempt twisting his face. "I own this town! I own the politicians and the bureaucrats! I own the law! You think this is anything but a minor inconvenience!?!"

"Haymer is talking to a state judge now," Holly's voice informed them. Adam spared a glance and saw that, of course, she had defied his orders. She and Peter, both astride the Beast, were back some small distance as Isandro's people and the Rangers were accepting surrenders. The bike, however, had obeyed, and kept his engine warm and his eyes pointed to an escape route, if needed. "She's saying the Rangers will take custody of Orobas. Isandro will take care of the Mayor. The Twins are posting all this online. They'll make sure everything Orobas did does national."

"Tell everyone..." Adam paused, an unfamiliar word tangling in his lips for a moment. "Tell all my... friends... thank you." He put the phone back into his coat pocket and stared at Orobas with a blank expression.

"You..." the Fallen Watcher shook with rage. He looked out to the grounds, where the cops loyal to him were already giving up their weapons. Orobas seemed as though he could feel his control slipping with the sudden exposure. A beeping from his coat caught his attention. He withdrew his own phone from an inner pocket and manipulated it, staring daggers at the screen. "Those little bitches!" he snarled. Looking at Adam, the Fallen Watcher who, for centuries, had protected himself with anonymity paled. "Everything I said! It's everywhere!"

"The Twins were always good and passing along gossip." His hard eyes turned to stone. "And don't ever call my little sisters bitches again."

"I CALL THEM WHATEVER I WANT, ZA'AFIEL!" Orobas roared. "I'll hunt them down! I'll torture them! I'll make them pay!" His entire body shook in rage. He pointed his gun at Adam, but it too shook violently. Even if the Fallen Watcher had any skill with weapons, his confusion and shock would have overwhelmed it. He took several breaths, looking around, flailing against the unplanned, the unexpected. "This... this... you'll... I'll..." He glanced at Chezef and then back at Adam. "You're still going to die! And so are all your women!"

With that, the great manipulator stormed off, down the broken staircase and back into the protective darkness, leaving the two brothers to their vendetta.

"You look just like I feel," Adam noted.

"Long night," Chezef replied. He glanced to the brightening horizon. "But it's just about done."

Adam reached into the pocket of his white leather coat and withdrew the stun gun Holly and the Twins had forced upon him. "I'm supposed to use this on you and escape," he told his brother. The warrior tossed the idiot technological thing over the side of the roof. He then slowly, deliberately, removed his white leather coat. He then drew his knife and meaningfully tossed it aside.

"Why?" Chezef asked.

Adam took a deep breath. "I'm honestly not sure. Maybe I think I deserve this. Maybe I think you deserve your revenge. Maybe..." The warrior gave a soft, rueful laugh. "Peter... Haziel, told me I always have to do something spectacular." He shrugged. "Maybe it's just that."

Mirroring his brother, Chezef sheathed his blades and removed his coat, tossing that aside before unbuckling the harnessed sheaths from his legs and tossing them as well. Adam noted without surprise that the damage to his vengeful brother was even worse when exposed. His shirt was in red tatters. Still-open wounds leaked onto his hard chest. A single glance revealed broken ribs. His entire, muscled torso was a patchwork of deep bruises, and a slight tremor kept the muscles in one arm twitching.

"Any chance I can talk you out of this?" Adam asked.

Chezef only stared hate at his brother.

Adam nodded towards where Orobas had retreated. "You know he's just using you."

"Does it seem like I care?"

Adam sighed, cracking his neck. "What happened..." he shook his head again. "What's done is done. It can't be undone. Even we, with all our power back in the day, even we couldn't unmake an action."

"Would you," Chezef asked without emotion. "If you could? Would you still obey Uriel. Would you still try to send me to the Pit?"

Adam looked again to the blushing sky. "If I had that kind of power..." he shook his head and looked down at his arms, seeing past the sleeves to the names carved upon his flesh. "There's a lot I'd change." The warrior turned back to the Fallen Angel of Destruction. "Do you know about Lilith?"

"I don't care."

"She's got nine of the Ten Pieces. She's assembling the Tetragrammaton. That's why the Tricksters brought me here. Why they brought you here. To try and save the last. To keep it from her." He stopped then, his hard eyes widening. Adam glanced back into the dark horizon and the fading lights of Disanté. "Son of bitch," he muttered.

"What?"

"The damned Tricksters," Adam was growling, then. "I gave up my blades to save Holly. I can't kill Lilith." The warrior looked at his vengeful brother, at the celestial weapons he had briefly set aside, but not forsaken. "But you've still got yours.

"I saved Peter from Orobas. I just wrecked the Watcher's control over this town. But Lilith's still going to come for him. That's why we didn't hear about Peter until Halloween; they needed time to get you here."

"Orobas sent me a message," Chezef noted.

"But why?" Adam waved an arm towards the city. "Those damned Tricksters! They wanted you here, someone with the skill and the weapons to defeat Lilith! And here you are!"

"Doesn't much matter," the Fallen said. "When you're gone, so am I."

"You'll send yourself to the Pit?" Adam asked. "Fall on your Blades?"

Chezef shrugged. "I've been waiting for all of Human history. I knew you'd Fall, sooner or later."

Adam looked back to the horizon, one more time. "You've got to stop her, brother."

"I don't give a shit about Lilith."

"Do you give a shit about this world!?!" Adam demanded. "You've been wandering down here for centuries! Haven't you learned to give the slightest shit about these people!?!"

"No."

"Then what the Hell was all this for!?!" Adam roared. "All the blood? All the death? Everything we've… everything I'VE done!?!" The warrior reached up and ripped back the sleeve of one arm, exposing the names carved into his flesh. "What was all this for, brother? Why did we kill all these people? Why did we cause all this destruction?

"We've known, our whole lives, that the Chorus has a plan. We've known there's some design at work. We've trusted in that."

"You trusted," Chezef corrected. "You and Uriel and Apollyon and all the others. Even when the rebellion kicked off, you still all believed so much you were willing to slaughter each other. I smelled the bullshit in all of that, so Uriel ordered my damnation." His cold, indifferent face cracked into a snarl of remembered betrayal. "And you believed so much you came for me."

"So what do you believe in?" Adam almost whispered.

"Not a damn thing. You fools can go on fighting each other. Let Lilith have the Ten Pieces. Let her remake the world. Let one of you kill her. I don't care."

"You've been alone too long, brother," the warrior noted. "You've forgotten…" Adam glanced to the south. "Do you remember that last mission we went on together?"

"Gault," Chezef grunted.

"We destroyed that entire civilization, because of those damned spears of theirs." Adam looked meaningfully at his brother. "Do you remember what happened?"

"Get to the point," the Fallen growled. "You saved my life; so what?"

"I saved you from the spear," Adam corrected. "That Human had you on the ground, and was about to stab one of those spears of theirs right into your gut. I stopped him; I saved you."

Chezef said nothing, only stared unforgiving hate at his betrayer.

"And do you remember what you said to me, afterwards? Anything. All I ever had to do was ask."

"So now you're calling in your marker?" the Fallen said flatly. "Now. Not during the Rebellion. Not when you came for me. Not in all the centuries I've been alone down here. Now."

"That's right," Adam confirmed. "Now."

"I'm not leaving," Chezef said flatly.

"I'm not asking that." Adam faced his brother, and everything that was between them. "I betrayed you. I was ordered to kill you, to purge you, and I tried. Uriel hated you for not siding with us in the Rebellion. I knew better; I tried to change his mind. But Uriel believed anyone who didn't fight with us was as good as any traitor. So, when he ordered me to end you, I tried.

"I won't deny it." Adam sighed and looked his brother in the eyes. "I can only apologize, and try to make it right. I'll stand. I'll give you want you want. But, I want something in return."

"What?"

"Stay here." He pointed up towards the New Moon. "Give me one full cycle."

Chezef glanced to the New Moon.

"If you kill me, don't just leave. Lilith will come for the boy. She's just waiting for him to be unprotected. Stay and deal with her. Protect the Twins. Protect my friends. Don't let the Mother of Demons win."

"I told you I don't give a shit-"

"I'm not asking you to give a shit," Adam interrupted. "I'm asking you for one Moon."

Chezef was silent, staring at his betrayer. Finally, "Fine. One Moon. When you die, I'll wait one Moon, and keep your little friends safe from Lilith and whatever else the Queen Bitch of Hell sends." The Fallen held up a finger. "But only for one Moon."

"Your word?"

The Fallen nodded. "I swear it."

Adam nodded. "Alright then." He cracked his neck. "Let's do this."

15

Both men were Fallen. They were both former Angels of Destruction. They were not creatures of deception. They were not strategists. Each of them had been spoken into being with a single, unsubtle purpose. They looked at each other, taking off their coats and loosening the sleeves of their shirts. They were both unbeatable warriors, but also they were men who had endured a long, hard night. They were equally beaten, equally broken, and equally exhausted. The brothers moved forward, without hurry, limping as much as walking, without any cursing or challenging or taunting. Everything that was to be said, had been said.

They stared at each other through blackened, bloody eyes, only a few breaths and a thousand regrets separating them.

Chezef punched Adam in the face.

Adam stumbled back, shaking his head to clear his vision. He wiped the fresh blood from his now re-broken nose. "That all you've got?"

"You wanna see what I've got!?!" Chezef snarled, advancing on Adam.

Adam punched Chezef in the face, much harder than his brother had punched him.

Chezef stumbled back, against the parapet wall lining the roof. He put his hand to his own nose and looked at the blood in growing fury.

"All these centuries," Adam said calmly. "All this time waiting to kick my ass, and this is what you show?" The warrior shook his head. "I think you're gonna be eatin' this roof before we're done, brother."

The two circled each other, arms raised and ready. Both knew every fighting style, every technique ever created. If a master of the martial arts were to see them, in that moment, though, the two brothers would have appeared as nothing more than brutish brawlers.

Adam swung a wide punch for his brother's chin. Chezef jerked his head back and darted forward, landing multiple blows to his brother's stomach, following up immediately with twin jabs to his bleeding nose. Adam fell to the roof floor, struggling to regain his breath. He lightly touched his face with a trembling hand and climbed back to his feet. Chezef took a step back, letting his brother stand again.

"Stop hitting my nose, asshole," Adam growled.

Chezef jabbed his fist towards Adam's face again, but his brother ducked under the strike, countering with rapid jabs to Chezef's chin. "It's already, fucking broken!" Adam barked between punches.

Chezef hit the floor but came back up almost immediately, spitting away thick red gobs. The Fallen shook his head clear, smiling through a mouth of broken teeth.

"Do we really have to do this?" Adam demanded, blocking a punch. "There's no point to this!" another blocked punch.

"Fight!" Chezef roared and threw his entire body into a punch.

Adam jerked to the side, letting the overthrown punch pass, and then he drove his fist in Chezef's scarred face. The Fallen did not collapse back to the roof floor, but was bent over for a moment. Adam walked up, beside his brother. "This is what they want!" he insisted

Chezef drove his elbow back, into Adam's chin. He then grabbed the back of Adam's burn-scarred head and drove his other elbow across his brother's jaw. Adam hit the floor hard but rolled immediately back to his feet, spitting blood and teeth and snarling his growing rage.

Chezef did not wait, did not allow his brother to steady himself, instead grabbing what was left of Adam's disheveled, now-burnt hair and jamming his fist into his brother's face.

Adam stayed on the roof floor for a moment. "This is gonna be a long fucking mornin'," he grumbled.

"We're just gettin' started," Chezef promised. He limped around Adam and grabbed his brother's hair again, lifting him up and raising his knee in preparation to further abuse Adam's already broken face.

Adam punched his brother in the crotch.

"You dirty mother-!"

Adam stepped in and jerked his head up, so that the back of his skull crashed into his brother's jaw. Chezef stumbled, but his brother held him up, only to drive the front of his skull into Chezef's face.

"This," Adam gasped. "Is what they want!" He stumbled a few steps back as his brother lay on the roof floor, regaining his breath. "This is what they ALWAYS want!" Adam pulled his brother back to his feet. "You fighting me! Me fighting you! Killing each other! Betraying each other! This is always THEIR GAME! Don't you get it!?!"

Chezef looked about to fall, but Adam reached forward to keep him upright. The Fallen suddenly jerked his knee up, into his brother's bloody face, and sending Adam back to the floor again.

"This shit's gittin' old."

Chezef stood a few paces away, his exhausted body weaving as he wearily stared contempt down at his brother. "You were always weaker, always so eager to help." The Fallen leaned in, just slightly. "We're not creatures of forgiveness, we've only ever been destroyers!"

In a blur of motion, Adam was back on his feet. He darted forward, grabbing his brother and driving his fist into Chezef's middle again and again and again. The force of each punch lifted the Fallen off the ground, banishing breath and causing and ejection of blood from the nose and mouth. As damaging as the blows were to Chezef, though, his brother felt the pain as well. His knuckles opened and his already-numb fists became little more than raw meat. Adam kept punching, kept swinging. Fists landed on Chezef's face, on his liver, his kidneys. Adam drove his brother up against the parapet wall, still landing blow after blow.

One tired punch drew Adam's arm too far back. Chezef blocked it and drove the base of his palm into his brother's sternum. Momentarily dazed, Adam stumbled back, but Chezef grabbed him, wrapping an arm around his brother's neck and pulling him down to received punch after upwards punch into the face. Adam grabbed the back of his brother's head, pulling back, even as he again punched Chezef in the crotch.

This time, Adam did not pause. The arm that was pulling back on Chezef's head then wrapped around the throat. The fist that had punished his brother's crotch swept up, behind Chezef's legs. With a great heave, Adam lifted the Fallen off the ground and twisted, driving his brother and himself down. Chezef hit the roof floor with a great woosh of lost air and a geyser of blood, a fraction of an instant before his hulking brother's mass came down on top of him.

They struggled on the ground, grabbing and twisting, kicking and gouging. Growling and cursing and spitting and biting brought news splashes of blood. Adam finally rolled on top of his brother and bodily grabbed Chezef, slamming the Fallen down into floor again and again. Adam pushed his thumb into his brother's bloody eye, bringing a growling scream. Chezef surged up, flinging his brother away.

Chezef did not wait, instead climbing on top of his brother. He drove his knee repeatedly into Adam's crotch. "How do you like it!?!" he roared before driving his own knuckle into his brother's bloody eye.

Adam used his leverage to roll Chezef off but could not follow up with an attack. What little strength remaining with him was fast seeping away, along with all the fluids his broken body leaked from its innumerable wounds. The two warriors gasped for air, struggling to regain their feet, to maintain their focus. Eventually, they regained their exhausted feet, facing each other, both warriors a mass of raw wounds.

Chezef punched Adam.

Adam punched Chezef.

Chezef reached back again and launched a punch, but Adam swung his off-hand up, capturing the attacking arm and twisting it. He pulled Chezef's arm back, behind his back and wrapped his other arm across his brother's throat. "How long!?!" Adam roared into his brother's ear. "How damned long are you going to keep being their toy!?! Their tool!?! Their little bitch!?!"

Chezef stomped on his brother's foot, causing Adam to lose his grip. The Fallen then picked his brother up and threw him to the ground. "I left the Chorus!" the Fallen roared, kicking his brother. "I left you!" another kick. "I left Uriel!" another kick. "I don't need any of you fuckers!" another kick. "I'm nobody's tool, nobody's weapon!" He stumbled back, near to the point of exhaustion.

Adam lay on the roof floor, just as exhausted. "Then," he gasped. "Why are… you… doing what… they want?"

Chezef stumbled back, against the parapet wall. "I do… what I want!" he insisted through gasps of air.

Adam tried to laugh. "When have you… EVER done what you want?" The warrior spit up a thick glob of red pain. "When have I?" He looked at his brother through a swelling, blood-coated eye. "I wanted to drink myself to death," he admitted through pain-filled pants. "I wanted to just be done. But then, a girl just happens to show up in my bar. She just happens to need help, that only I can give." More attempted laughter. "Sound familiar, brother?"

Adam forced himself to sit up, dismissively spitting aside another thick glob that tasted as though it was once part of an important organ. "How many times, brother?" he asked wearily. "You've been down here for centuries." Adam stared at Chezef. "How many times have you been 'doing what you want' and something comes along? You just happen to come across a Dark Angel, a Fallen, or some damned rogue Daimon? Some problem, that only you could fix, just happens to cross your path." Adam tried again to laugh. "How many times?"

Chezef stared at his brother for a long while. He then looked off to the rising Dawn. "Son of a bitch," he muttered, sitting against the parapet wall.

"It's what they do," Adam confirmed. "It's what they are." The warrior stood, slowly, painfully, reluctantly. "They drew me here. For all I know, they were involved in that mess in London. They're afraid of Lilith, but there's no way they'll fight her themselves, not when they can get a couple of Fallen Angels of Destruction to do it for them."

Adam picked up Chezef's blades, being careful to only touch the straps. He walked over to his brother and handed the weapons over. "I'm too fuckin' tired to keep doin' this. If you want to go on being their little pet…" Adam waved at the blades. "Go ahead. I'm done with their games."

"How do you know?" Chezef asked as Adam was turning away.

"What?" he brother asked.

"How do you know you're not just doing more of what they want?"

Adam shrugged. "Hell if I know," he admitted. "I'm not trying to outthink a Trickster. All I know is, there are people I give a shit about. The Twins, Holly, Candace. I've got people who are important to me, who count on me to protect them. Haziel… Peter is my… he's our little brother. He's protecting the last free Piece of the Tetragrammaton. To get it, Lilith has to kill him. Our little brother became a Fallen to keep it away from her. You, me. All the others. We all became Fallen for ourselves."

"That's not why you Fell," Chezef pointed out.

Adam stared at him.

His Fallen brother snorted. "Yeah, I heard. Some of them still talk to me, still try to… fuck, I don't even know why." Chezef stared at Adam. "Simkiel told me what happened at you trial… at your acquittal. He told me why you really Fell."

"It doesn't matter," Adam growled.

"Doesn't it?"

"It's all bullshit anyway!" the warrior barked. "All of it! Why you Fell! Why I Fell! It's all bullshit! None of it matters!" Adam ripped open his shirt, exposing the names, all of his sins, to the new day. "THIS is what matters! It has to mean something!"

Chezef stared at Adam's chest, at one point, right over his brother's heart.

"Yeah," the warrior grunted. "Your name. You were the first." Adam collapsed back to the ground, needing all his remaining strength just to sit somewhat straight. "You were first, and that shit has to matter." Adam shook his head. "If Peter dies, he goes to the Pit. Sooner or later, the Queen Bitch of Hell is going to come for him. She's going to try to kill him. My friends are going to try to stop her, to protect Peter. Lilith will kill them to get to our little brother. You, me," Adam gestured to the names forever carved into his body. "All of this has to have been for something."

Adam forced himself to stand, however unsteadily. He stared at Chezef. "You and me, all the Angels of Destruction, we were all spoken into being creatures of violence. Most of our brothers never questioned that. You did. You tried to walk away, but they won't let you. You've still spent all these centuries doing their work. It was the same for me. I tried to walk away, but they pulled be back in."

Adam walked towards the broken stairwell and paused. "We were looking for something, brother. I realize that now. You and me, we were both looking. I found something worth fighting for. What about you?"

The Fallen said nothing for a moment. He stayed, leaning against the parapet wall, looking from his brother to the horizon and back. Finally, Chezef was about to speak, but was interrupted. Bullet tore up from the roof floor. The shots were not near the Fallen, though, but instead surrounded his brother.

Adam screamed as shot after shot lanced up, through the roof. His feet were pierced, again and again, shredding the boots and the flesh within. The warrior fell back, blood pooling around him.

Orobas charged back onto the roof through the broken stairwell. The Fallen Watcher still had his pistol, but the slide was locked back and the barrel smoked. "I'm ruined, you pathetic reject! Years, centuries of work gone in a night!" He laboriously ejected the weapon's magazine and struggled to replace it with fresh rounds.

"And you!" the Fallen Watcher glanced contemptuously at Chezef. "You had one job! The one thing you've wanted to do for centuries! Just kill him! How hard is that!?!" Orobas finally got the new magazine loaded and was struggling to release the slide as he walked towards the groaning Adam. "What good are any of you morons?" the Fallen Watcher was muttering. "You can't even do as your told! You're pathetic!"

Orobas reached Adam's side and finally managed to get his weapon ready, orienting it towards Adam's face. "You think you've won something?" he demanded. "You really think this is some kind of victory? Lilith is still coming, you idiot! She's going to rip that Piece right out of the boy! If you're lucky, she'll just kill your little friends! You know her." He glanced back towards Chezef. "Both you fools know her! She's merciless! She corrupts everything she touches!" Orobas looked back down at Adam. "Is that what you wanted? Huh? I would have just taken the boy and been done with it. She won't stop! She'll make you watch as she corrupts your friends, as she turns them into whores and addicts! What the Hell were you thinking!?!"

"Right now," Adam grunted through the pain and the loss of blood. "Right now, I'm thinking, 'he's really screwed.'"

Orobas looked confused for a moment, but then his eyes widened at the sound of Celestial weapons being freed. The Fallen Watcher glanced at Chezef, but saw only an Angel of Destruction, advancing on him. "No!" Orobas screamed, firing at his murderer. "No! No!"

Chezef casually deflected each shot with his blades. He did not break his steady stride, did not pause for uneven terrain. His eyes were locked upon his target.

Orobas backed away, firing and screaming and begging and cursing. He weapon once more clicked empty, the slide terminally locked. The Fallen Watcher dropped the useless hunk of technology and kept backing away. "Please!" he uselessly begged. "I've got power, wealth, influence! I can give you anything!" He bumped against the distant parapet wall. "We've both walked this world for centuries! You know the pleasures that can be found here!"

"I've never found any." Chezef's voice was empty. An echo of the Pit was all the sound that came from the advancing Angel of Destruction as he raised his blades.

Orobas, the chunks of him, were sent screaming over the edge of the building, and hurtling into the Pit.

16

The door to Adam's bedroom banged open. Holly, her bright face framed with an oversized Santa hat, shouted, "Merry Christmas!" while joyously shaking a string of sleigh bells. Her blue pajamas with silver snowflakes sown in looked frumpy and wrinkled. This, along with her unkempt hair spoke of just having risen from bed. For once, it seemed to Adam, his little friend had made no effort at "making herself presentable."

Behind Holly, looking a little confused but not unhappy stood Peter. The previous night, she had forced on the newest member of their family a pair of similar, holiday-themed pajamas, these cheerful red with candy canes and reindeer. Though the Fallen Cherub quite obviously did not understand all of Holly's commandments for the holiday, he had complied without complaint.

In response to the early-morning invasion, Adam tried grumbling and pulling the blankets further over his head. Not to be denied, however, Holly ran to his side of the bed and forcibly pulled back the warm covers. "Wake up, sleepy head!" she cheerfully commanded. The young woman then nearly danced to the window and drew back the heavy curtains. "Look what Santa brought!"

Adam, morning light stabbing into his eyes, looked and was unimpressed.

Through the large double windows lay the Twins ranch. The large pasture was empty, the animals having been stabled and the hands sent home with extra pay. Private security still patrolled the grounds, as they had for the three weeks since Orobas' defeat. The men were hard professionals, trained and equipped and utterly loyal to the Twins. The unyielding black of their clothes and gear contrasted sharply against the snow.

Winter had at last come in full force that night. As though the clouds had descended upon Meropis County, a heavy blanket lay upon the world. Wet snow clung to everything, an adornment for each branch, roof, vehicle, and hill. The quiet storm had not lingered, though. The sky was a clear, brilliant sea stretching from one horizon to the other. Rosy Dawn declared the arrival of Christmas morning with a golden canvas traced with scarlet ribbons adorning the last retreating clouds.

"So pretty!" Holly beamed. As a child of Texas, she held special joy when gifted a winter wonderland, most especially when that gift came on Christmas.

"Oooo," Adam grunted non-committaly.

Holly spun and punched him in the shoulder, making sure to hit the solid one and not the shoulder that still bore deep bruises. "Get up, Grinch!" she commanded.

Candace roused herself beside Adam and sat up. "We'll be along presently," she promised sleepily. Her great mass of auburn hair flared out like a lion's mane, feral and pure. Only one strand had detached from the chaotic halo, having stuck itself to the side of her face. Candace had made no announcement, nor had she consulted with Adam. After his discharge from the hospital, Candace had simply begun sleeping in what was supposed to be his bed. The warrior had wanted to object, to demand his earned privacy, but the first night of having her lying beside him, her head on his chest, her hand over his heart, and her legs intwined with his, had banished any possible resistance.

He had even gotten used to the frequency with which her auburn hair writhed itself into his mouth each night.

Holly danced away from the bed, content in their obedience. She took Peter's hand and led him down the hallway, either forgetting or not caring to close the door.

Candace leaned over and placed a gentle kiss on Adam's cheek. "Merry Christmas," she murmured into his ear. "Let's get you moving," she said, rising

Adam growled and grumbled his indignant surrender. As ever, though, his eyes remained fixed on her as she rose. Candace, as had become her habit, had worn one of his t-shirts to bed. She moved to the large wooden dresser along the wall opposite the windows. The former bartender retrieved a few things and went to the bathroom, partially closing the door. This, also, had become her habit. Adam still had not seen Candace without clothes in full light; she insisted on changing outside of his view, or in darkness.

With the Waystation gone, so too was any source of income for Candace. She had shed no tears for the loss of the bar, unlike Adam, who had held on to a dim hope that he could one day return to the safety of its bottles and its delicious oblivion. He had offered to give Candace whatever money she needed, but the former bartender had firmly rebuffed the handout. Instead, the Twins had officially hired her as Adam's caretaker during his recovery, paying the woman far better than anything the Waystation had offered. Candace had taken to her new duties with a quiet, graceful zealotry.

When she returned, Candace was wearing plaid pajama bottoms that matched those Adam was wearing, as well as a large grey sweatshirt that, in red calligraphy across her ample chest, said, "Naughty-ish." She sat in one of the upholstered chairs and put on thick socks before moving to Adam's side. "Ready?" she asked.

"Does it matter?" he grumbled in response.

Candace smiled and kissed his other cheek before retrieving the wheelchair. She brought this beside the bed and locked the brakes. One of her surprisingly-strong arms looped under his legs and helped spin them towards the floor. Her house had survived that long night, remaining strangely untouched by Orobas' schemes. She still had her own bed, her own closets, her own everything. Adam glanced around as she guided him into the wheelchair. His closet here, his dresser and his bathroom, contained more her Candace's possessions than his own. In the weeks since they had moved into the Ranch, she had not quite taken up full residence, but whatever distinction there could be, Adam remained ignorant.

"I can do this, you know," Adam said, not un-gently. His recovery was well under way. Though the doctors had insisted he would need at least six weeks to even begin regaining the use of his feet, the warrior was already wearing normal shoes and socks again. He was even scheduled to begin his physical therapy the following week.

"I don't mind," Candace said softly. "It is my job, after all." She pulled thick wool socks over his scarred feet, one at a time. Her touch was as gentle as spring mist, bringing no discomfort to the ugly puncture scars. Several surgeries had been needed, with specialists rerouting nerves and blood vessels, installing small bone and skin grafts, and constant rounds of cleaning. Despite all their work, or perhaps because of it, Adam's feet were an ugly twisting of scars. The warrior, as he often did when looking at his damaged feet, glanced also to his hands. The burn scars on his left hand, and the hole in his right hand from the Gault Spear seemed somehow to match. One hand wandered to his nose and mouth. After multiple breakings, the scars around his nose would not fade, he knew. Dental surgeries had repaired his teeth, granting modern replacements that were nearly indistinguishable from the real thing, but something of a pain to keep clean.

Candace noticed Adam's frown and to where his attention drifted. "Don't worry at it," she told him, not for the first time.

"We heal fast," the warrior told her. He had said the same thing, when he had awoken in the hospital to see her at his bedside. Holly and Peter had been sleeping in a different chair, and the Twins had been out in the hall, calling in their preferred doctors and surgeons.

"Fallen can heal most injuries," Adam said as Candace pulled what she called house-shoes over his damaged feet. "Our bodies are tough. We're almost immortal. But there are limits."

"I know," she said without looking up.

He reached down and lifted her chin, raising her soft eyes to his hard ones. "It's barely been six months," he insisted. "Most Fallen spend centuries without serious injury. If they're careful, their bodies won't ever wear out." He held up his scarred hands. "I'm not careful."

Candace enfolded his scarred hands in her gentle ones. "Keep bein' the man you are," she told him. "Don't let anyone make you change." She ducked her head under his shoulder and leveraged him into the wheelchair, then arranged his legs into the raised stirrups.

"Besides you, you mean?" he said sourly. "And Holly. And the Twins. And-"

"It's Christmas," Candace said with a flick of a finger across his bent nose. "Don't be such a sourpuss."

The living room, in short order, had become a mess of discarded wrapping paper. The great, living tree in the center of the room glittered with holiday cheer, adorned with pure white lights and garland and decorations of every kind. During Adam's stay in the hospital, Holly and the Twins had peremptorily moved everyone into the Ranch. Whatever meager possessions that survived Orobas' bomb were retrieved and brought to their new home. Holly and Peter were each assigned their own rooms beside one another, even as a third was prepared by Candace for her and Adam. The bartender still had her house, and kept many of her possessions there, but most of her time was now spent at the ranch.

In her role as the mistress of her new domain, Holly had overseen the acquisition of a Christmas Tree. The decorating of it had been the first order of business upon Adam's discharge from the hospital. Though most of the night was spent with the women clustered around the poor tree, happily chattering amongst themselves and draping one another in glittering garland while Adam and Peter helpfully held ornaments pending their deployment.

The Twins took to Holly's enthusiastic holiday cheer with relish. The days following Orobas' long night were especially hard on them. When the former City Manager had bombed their office building, several of their employees had been killed. The Twins had insisted on attending each funeral, visiting with each family, and sharing in the mourning. Adam's release from the hospital, and Holly and Peter's moving into their ranch, had been the only light in their lives for a long while.

"We could run, you know," Adam had whispered to Peter, low enough that their jailors would not hear.

"Too late," the boy had smiled with a nod to his immobilized legs.

Gifts had also been one of Holly's commandments. They had each opened one, as per the empress' command, on Christmas Eve. This had happened after Candace, with Adam nearby, had lit the candles in her yule log, and whispered a soft prayer. "Asking for anything in particular?" Adam had asked.

The former bartender had only glanced at him and smiled. "Nothing I don't already have."

She had given him a new knife that night, a large Bowie with a bone handle and blade so bright and sharp it seemed to cut the air itself. Adam had tested it, and the blade was perfectly balanced. A dara knot was inscribed in red on the bone handle. Candace had stared at him as he marveled the fine blade, and the slight upturn of her lips grew with his own happiness with the gift.

After carefully returning his new knife to its sheath, Adam had handed Candace a small box. From this, the former bartender withdrew the small object within and gave a startled, delighted gasp.

"A bear?" Holly had asked in curiosity.

Candace held with near reverence a small carving of a black bear, the same one she had admired at the Tree Lighting Festival. "Thank you," she whispered, placing a gentle kiss upon Adam's cheek.

Even with the single gifts opened the night before, Christmas morning still beheld a great avalanche of presents. Holly squealed in delight when she opened her gift from the Twins. As far as Adam could tell, they were just shoes, but the women all looked almost lustfully at the foot wear as Holly replaced her fuzzy slippers, holding her feet into the air and staring in wide-eyed adoration of the shoes.

"Shouldn't you walk around in them?" Adam asked. "See if they're comfortable?"

Each of the women stared at him as though he were some inarticulate primate playing in his own feces.

Adam opened his gift from Holly and tried to seem pleased with the large, black disk, but could not find the words. "Johnny Cash?" was all he thought to say.

"Yeah," she said. "Let's try getting your music tastes at least to the last hundred years."

"I think you'll like him," Candace added. "You'll… understand him."

"What's this?" Holly asked then, having carefully opened her gift from Adam.

"*Méthode Compléte de Harpe*," he answered. "By-"

"Henriette Renié," the young woman finished, her voice awestruck.

"Her writing is mostly for larger instruments," Adam warned.

"But the technique is the same," Holly replied, her large, dark eyes lost in the pages of the old book."

The Twins also received books from Adam. Nicolas Sparks, *The Notebook* for Marun, and Emily Brontë's *Wuthering Heights* for Harun. Both sisters squealed in delight over the first edition stories, and held their respective gifts reverently.

They all showered Peter with toys. The Fallen Cherub opened these and was emphatic in his gratitude, making sure each gift-giver was delighted in their feeling of generosity. Though, in each case, Peter shared a confused look with Adam. The warrior, for his part, tried to be a little more understanding of his little brother.

"You like Emily Dickinson?" Holly asked, looking out from the great mass of ribbons adorning her head. With each gift, she had carefully untied the ribbon and placed it either around her narrow shoulders or over the oversized Santa hat upon her head. She sat beside Peter as they unwrapped their presents, taking even more joy in the Cherub's gifts than her own.

Peter lifted the small, leather-bound book from its box. His small fingers drifted along the engraved title and author. "Her life wasn't easy," he almost whispered. "Full of… I tried so hard to help her." He looked to Adam. "Thank you, brother."

Adam nodded, understanding the feeling of trying to help a mortal, and failing.

Candace retrieved a box from under the large tree and presented it to Adam, returning to her place beside him on one of the couches. "Open mine," she instructed.

He ripped apart the wrapping paper and lifted what was inside. "A vest?" he asked, confused. It was brown leather, broad to accommodate his thick chest, and tapered as it fell.

Candace slid even closer, her eyes on the vest. "I think you'd look good in it," she almost purred with an edge of rising heat in her voice. "Just like a true gunfighter." Her finger almost absently traced through his newly-cut hair. The leg closest to him slid just a bit up and down against his frame.

"Uh, ok. Thank you." Adam was confused, and glanced at Holly. She stared commands at him, instructions that she had painstakingly gone over the night before, in preparation for receiving Candace's gift. "Maybe I can wear it tonight?" he suggested as he had been instructed.

Candace smiled warmly, the heat in her voice rising to her eyes. "That would be… very nice."

"Open his!" Holly demanded, retrieving a small box from under the tree and almost dancing to the couch. She presented the gift with its simple wrapping and small green bow as though it were a laurel wreath of victory.

Candace accepted the small gift and carefully unwrapped it, skillfully pulling at the corners and preserving the paper, which she folded and set aside. The former bartender then opened the box, her soft green eyes going wide at what lay inside and a gasp escaping her lips.

"What is it?" the Twins demanded.

Candace lifted the pendant from its box. The chain was of rose gold, a seemingly-delicate chain of uniform links. The emerald was shaped into a heart, and caught the glittering lights of the Christmas Tree and the cheerful fireplace, mesmerizing each of the women. Around the emerald-heart was a diamond shaped in such a way as to seem as though the one gem was enfolding the other in a tight embrace. Candace stared at the pendant with wide eyes and an open mouth, lost in her avarice for the gift and what it represented.

Adam glanced again at Holly, who pursed her lips and jerked her head slightly. The warrior took the pendant. "May I?" he asked as he had been told to.

Candace nodded and turned slightly, lifting her great mane to expose the back of her neck.

Adam carefully, leaning on the many practice sessions upon which Holly had insisted, worked the tiny chain's tiny latch. His damaged fingers trembled slightly as he forced them to bend, almost more than they were now able. Finally, he draped the adornment around Candace's neck, so that the pendant hung just below her collar bone. Although it had not been part of the rehearsals, some instinct took charge of Adam, and he laid a light kiss to the back of Candace's neck. Beneath his lips and the press of the diamond-enfolded emerald, the former bartender's skin shuddered, almost writhed, her breath coming short and her every muscle filling with tension.

Candace let her auburn hair fall and tuned back, her eyes going from the pendant to Adam. The women oooed and aahed the decoration, while Peter continued looking nearly as confused as Adam felt. Candace leaned in to kiss Adam, seemingly meaning for it to be tender, but her breathing came heavier as her urge rose. She pressed into him, her hands gripping into his shirt and his flesh.

This went on for some time. Finally, Holly said, "So, who wants to try out his new sled?"

The day was spent at play. Holly and Peter took turns riding his new sled down the steep hill behind the ranch's main house. The Twins brough out new snowmobiles for everyone to ride upon. The Beast joined in their cavorting through the snowy hills encompassing much of the ranch. An entire family of snowmen were built, one for each of them, including the motorcycle. The pool was obviously unusable, but the Twins arranged for a temporary ice rink, and taught the Texan girls how to skate. Adam and the Beast looked on, both of whose wheels made ice too risky a prospect. As the day began to pass, Candace led the preparation of a great feast, taking advantage of the Twins' huge, well-appointed kitchen.

As the meal was nearing readiness, Isandro and Haymer arrived. The pair insisted that they had arrived separately, and with no prior coordination, but Holly looked skeptical, especially given that only one car sat in the driveway. She ignored their objections at placing the two beside one another at the table, though these protests faded quickly. Adam was placed at the head of the table, and instructed in carving the turkey for them all, a task for which he relied heavily on Candace, seated to his side. Holly, on his other side, led them in a simple prayer before helping with the distribution of the food.

"How's your department doing?" Adam asked Isandro.

The good cop grimaced. "Still struggling with patrols," he admitted. The lieutenant, whose unit had been the only one unaffected by the recent purge, threw a mockingly-harsh glare at Haymer. "Frankie here was pretty damned thorough."

"Stop hiring corrupt assholes," the tall Ranger shrugged. Under her leadership, Haymer had spent the past weeks gathering up the men who had aided Orobas in his night of mayhem. This included a great many cops, leaving Disanté's peace officers dangerously understaffed. She started, then, and glanced guiltily at Peter. "Excuse my French."

"I'm thousands of years old," the Fallen Cherub pointed out. "I was there when swearing was invented."

"Good job with that," Adam grunted towards the Twins.

"We were just helping them express themselves," Harun insisted.

"It's not our fault Humans have such dirty minds," Marun sniffed.

"We put in a request to Austin for replacements from other towns," Isandro continued, as always wanting to keep the conversation away from things his Catholicism was ill-equipped to handle. "We'll get by."

"It's strange there hasn't been an uptick in crime," Haymer noted. "You'd think, with less cops on the streets, the animals would take advantage."

"We've gotten reports of a vigilante," Isandro said. "Someone's going after the scum. Drug dealers, pimps, muggers. Anyone who steps out of line catches one hell of a beating. Sometimes worse."

"Chezef," Harun said with a mix of sadness and speculation.

"He's experimenting," Marun added.

"With what?" Candace asked.

"With giving a shit." The Twins looked meaningfully at Adam, who shrugged.

"Give him time," the warrior advised. "He'll either settle down, or something big will catch his attention."

"You know," Isandro pointed out, "he did assault a lot of cops."

"How many of them are in jail, now?"

"Not the point," the good cop insisted. "He needs to answer for his crimes."

"Believe me," Adam said, "he does."

"Will you two reopen your agency?" Haymer asked Holly.

"Eventually," she replied through a full mouth. Holly jerked her head towards Adam. "This one won't be much use until his feet heal. There haven't been any calls on the agency line, lately. Once he's back up, though, we'll reopen."

The dinner and the light conversation continued. Dessert came out, a mixture of pies and pastries that had everyone groaning by the end, content in their feast. Eventually, after the clean-up was finished, they all gathered in the living room, warmed by the cheerful fire and their company. After much urging, Holly brough out her harp, and played for them a number of carols, to which Candace and Haymer added their voices. After a time, they all joined in.

Dusk came. None of them made any effort to leave, nor was any suggestion offered. The Twins casually pointed out the spare bedrooms, and offered both Isandro and Haymer their welcome. An unasked question drifted for a time, as to how many extra rooms would be needed.

The good cheer of the holiday was interrupted at the same moment the sun slipped behind the distant hills. Adam was the first to sense it, though Peter and the Twins stiffened soon after. Their eyes went to the patio and the covered pool beyond. There, standing and waiting, was Chezef.

Isandro and Haymer, picking up on the rising tension from the Fallen Angels, let their hands drift to their service weapons, but Adam shook his head. "He's not here for that," the warrior declared. With Candace's help, he left the couch and regained his wheelchair. "Stay here."

Adam rolled to the back doors. Chezef stepped back, away from the house, giving his brother plenty of safe room. When he exited, Adam purposefully closed the door, preventing anyone from following, casting a hard look at Holly, who was already starting to sneak towards the kitchen door.

"Brother," Adam said to Chezef.

"I'm leaving," the Fallen Angel of Destruction said.

Adam glanced towards the waning moon. "You said you'd give me a full cycle."

Chezef shook his head. "I said I'd stay if you died. You didn't die, so I'm not staying."

"It takes time, brother," Adam said, as gently as his hard voice would allow. "You've only been at it a few weeks. And you've been going at it alone."

Chezef glanced behind Adam, at the people gathered in that warm living room amidst all the holiday cheer. The Fallen shook his head. "That might work for you, but…"

"You could come in," Adam offered. "You'd be welcome."

"We're not there," Chezef said darkly. "Not yet. Maybe not ever. You betrayed me. You did it because Uriel told you to. That's still between us."

Adam nodded. "Like I said," he paused, glancing behind at his friends and family. "Like I was told, I can only try to make it right today."

"Not now," Chezef said. "Maybe someday, but not now."

"Lilith's still out there," Adam pointed out. "She still wants the Piece Peter has. She won't just give up."

"Still not sure I give a damn. Maybe… I don't know."

Both the warriors paused then. They stared at each other, unfamiliar with what they were feeling. Adam glanced inside and noticed that Peter and the Twins were also agitated. Peter looked up and pointed, directing Adam and Chezef's eyes to the sky.

A great, sparking fireball was arcing down. It shone with all the colors, both seen and unseen, real and imagined. It shot from on high, banished from the Silver City and rocketed towards the flawed Earth below. The fireball impacting the Twin's covered pool and sent a great torrent of nearly-frozen water arcing up to soak the patio.

Adam, restricted by his injuries, could not rise. Chezef was not so encumbered, though. The Fallen Angel of Destruction leapt into the pool and retrieved the new arrival. He swam down, grabbing and pulling, hauling the body up to the edge of the icy pool.

"Simkiel!?!" Adam was shocked at the appearance of the now-Fallen Watcher.

Simkiel was nude, as they all were when they transubstantiated. The new wounds on his back, where his wings had just been cut away, still smoked, as did the crown of his head, where his halo had been destroyed. Simkiel blinked in confusion, lost in the extreme trauma of being forced into mortal flesh and banished forever from the Silver City. Adam and Chezef glanced at each other, both familiar with the horror of transubstantiation.

"Stir up the fire!" Adam called back into the house. "Blankets, dry clothes, warm drink! Now!"

Chezef was pulling at Simkiel, half-dragging the nearly-unconscious Watcher towards the house. Adam did what he could from his wheelchair, which was little. Simkiel's eyes fluttered, then fixed on Adam. When this happened, the Watcher tore free from Chezef and half-collapsed into Adam's lap.

"Lilith!" Simkiel screamed. "Za'afiel, Lilith is...!" his voice became choked amidst tears and horror and regret.

"We know," Adam said as soothingly as he was able. "We know she's coming."

"NO!" Simkiel shouted. "Lilith is here!"

Amen

Adam and Holly
continue their adventures
in
Redeeming Love

ABOUT THE AUTHOR

William Price Jr has never settled into any one role. He has been a teacher, a delivery truck driver, a soldier, a firefighter, and an editor. He has lived in California, Colorado, Texas, and now New England. Writing has been the only constant in his life, as he struggles to either maintain his sanity, or put it out of his misery.

www.ingramcontent.com/pod-product-compliance
Lightning Source LLC
LaVergne TN
LVHW040220110826
845146LV00005B/1356